Badlands Feud

The frontiers of the West were being pushed back rapidly as a whole nation began to move towards the promised land of California, a country of warm skies and gold for the taking. But, first, there were three thousand miles of desert and mountains to be crossed, rivers in full flood and hostile plains that stretched unbroken for hundreds of miles. Nevertheless the challenge produced a breed of men capable of meeting these dangers, men of vision who saw the country as something greater than a mere narrow eastern strip.

However, the pioneer had to have a repeating rifle if he was to be sure of fighting off attacks from hostile Indians and outlaws and it was not long before the Spencer, favourite arm of the Union cavalryman in the Civil War, was supplanted by the Henry, later developing into the most famous rifle of them all – the Winchester.

This is an inspiring novel of the development of this weapon, and of the men who conquered the West.

Badlands Feud

Randall Payne

A Black Horse Western

ROBERT HALE · LONDON

© 1964, 2002 John Glasby
First hardcover edition 2002
Originally published in paperback as
Badlands Feud by Chuck Adams

ISBN 0 7090 7219 8

Robert Hale Limited
Clerkenwell House
Clerkenwell Green
London EC1R 0HT

Typeset by
Derek Doyle & Associates, Liverpool.
Printed and bound in Great Britain by
Antony Rowe Limited, Wiltshire

ONE

High Stakes

The steamboat which had been tied up at the levee for more than three days, disgorging passengers and taking on the bales of cotton, was now ready to move away, out into the middle of that vast river, the Mississippi. Tracey Dillman had ridden into New Orleans five days before, riding down from the north, from Memphis, a disillusioned man who had fought for his state, had fought for what he believed to be right, only to have finished on the losing side after the hard, terrible years in which a nation had turned against itself, brought itself to the brink of ruin and was now trying to patch up the pieces, hoping to learn to live with itself and the memory of Civil War.

During these long years, he had learned many things which came only to a man in time of war, had seen his companions killed on all sides, while death had passed close to him without touching; not physically that is, but it had touched him in other ways, had burned a scar in his soul which would never heal. Now he was riding south, hoping to find a trail there which would lead him west, across three thousand miles of wilderness to the new state of California.

Battle-weary, he had checked his mount at the hotel which overlooked the river and now, with the early morning mists lying over the water, he could make out the great steamer getting ready to pull away, the vast wheel churning at the water, flinging it in shining cascades into the air where the sunlight caught the glittering drops and held them suspended behind the boat. There was all of the usual excitement down on the levee which attended a departure, a crowd milling on the quayside. Noise and laughter swelled from the narrow street below his window. Standing there, feeling the sun warm on his shoulders, he managed to forget a few of the aches and bruises in his own body, the hardness and lumpiness of the mattress on the bed which had given him restless nights in spite of the weariness in him.

Lifting his head, he glanced up, shading his eyes against the glare of the rising sun. The steamer was well away from the levee now, pulling out into midstream. Several people crowded the rails on the decks, waving to those behind on the bank. The departing whistle sounded with a mournful wail that carried to him and for a moment, he wished he was on board that vessel, going back along the way he had come. Then he thrust the thought away, putting it out of his mind. He realized that he was hungry and tightening the gunbelt around his middle, he left his room and made his way down the creaking, rickety stairs to the dining-room on the ground floor of the hotel.

Several of the tables were occupied but his was next to the windows where he could look out on to the street and watch the colourful procession that came from the quayside. A tall Negro came to his elbow and he gave his order, sitting back and forcing himself to relax. There was sure to be some wagon train moving out west, he told himself, as he waited for his breakfast. This town was one of the favourite jumping off points and many of them would hire their riders here, possibly needing a scout to ride with them across all of those hundreds of uncharted miles which lay between them and California.

He knew he could never remain here in the state which had once been his home. There were too many memories here of the days before the war between the States, but perhaps out there far to the west, he might be able to forget and find some place where he could put down roots.

Sitting with all of his muscles loose, fully enjoying the sheer laziness of the comfort, he ate his breakfast when it came, bacon and eggs, fried potatoes and sweet bread followed by hot, black coffee. When he had finished draining the second cup of coffee, he remained where he was, the energy of the meal a stimulant to him as he built himself a smoke. He had seen a lot of this town during the past five days, had seen some of the changes which had been wrought here by the war, but already, trade was coming back, although the men from the North were descending on the towns of the Mississippi like vultures, bleeding the people dry, doing it all in the name of America. Apart from the crooked politicians who were at the back of it all, determined that the South would have to pay as the defeated nation, there were the others who came, professing to be business men working for the South yet intent only on making money for themselves at the expense of others.

There were some of these men in this room, he knew, letting his gaze wander over the men at the other tables. It was relatively easy to pick them out in their black, close-fitting suits and expensive cigars, the way they threw their money around and expected everyone to come running to their beck and call.

He felt some of the old restlessness bubble up inside him as he sat there, listening to the multitude of sounds outside in the street, and images of his past drifted in front of his inner vision, the days before the war when he had ridden the wide trails that criss-crossed this state, when there had been none of this strange feeling of indifference which seemed to plague him now. The feeling of deep satisfaction evoked by the shimmering starlight which one saw only in the vast darknesses of the plains, the faint singing of the wind through cactus and mesquite,

and the tall, purple-shrouded mountains that lifted in
mystery on a skyline one never really seemed to reach no
matter how far you rode.

Those had been the carefree days of his youth. But he
had grown to manhood in the fires and thunder of war, in
the slaughter of men, the long marches, the rattle of
musket fire and the booming roar of the cannons, the
shriek of wounded animals and the smell of death. There
had been an insanity if men in those terrible days had
known what they were doing in the red swirl of battle, in
the cruel and merciless business of destroying their fellow
men. Whether they had known what they were doing or
not, he did not know. But now that it was all over, the ruthless and merciless business of bleeding the South dry still
went on and there was no one who would stand up and do
anything to stop it.

There was a sudden movement in the doorway of the
dining-room and Tracey glanced up, interested. The man
who stood there was short, stocky, well-built around the
shoulders, with hard eyes that drifted slowly about the
crowded room, passing over the faces of the men there
like a hurrying shadow thrown by the sun, then the glance
reached him, held for a long moment, passed on and then
swung back. The man came over to his table, stood there
for a second looking down at him, then motioned towards
the other, empty chair.

'Mind if I sit down, mister?' he asked.

'Sure, go ahead,' Tracey nodded.

The dark eyes narrowed a little as the other lowered
himself into the chair. He let his gaze wander over the grey
uniform which Tracey wore, but there was no sneering
malice in his look as there had been with so many men
Tracey had met these last few weeks.

The trace of a smile grew on the other's lips. 'You look
like a man who needs an aim in life, friend,' he said softly,
'Am I right?'

'Yes, you're right,' Tracey nodded. 'Do you consider
that you can provide me with that aim?'

'Perhaps.' The smile broadened a little, reached the man's eyes. 'You know there are wagon trains moving west all the time now that the war is over. There's little here for men of vision, but out there to the west lies the richest land of all and everybody is aiming to get there, some for the gold, others just to settle. A lot aren't going to make it. There are too many things against them. The country they have to cross for one; Indians and outlaws for another, coyotes and mountain lions. Nature hasn't been kind when she shaped the deserts that lie between us and the Pacific.'

'And you're offering me a job with a wagon train heading west?' said Tracey quietly.

'That's right. I need a man who has the courage to face everything we'll find there, a man who knows what it is to fight, even when the odds are against him.'

'And what makes you think that you'll get through where the others have failed?'

'That's a fair question,' said the other at long length. 'I figure it's all a matter of planning. These other settlers are moving out without any idea of the dangers they're likely to find. I've ridden some of that country to the west. I know what lies out there.'

'And you still think you can take a train through?'

'I'm positive I can. I've also arranged for a stock of those fancy rifles we used in the cavalry, Spencers.' Tracey nodded. He remembered those arms from his days in the war, the favourite weapon of the Union Cavalry. Some kind of repeater action if he recalled rightly. Not a perfect mechanism by a long way, but it might have an advantage over the others in use. He did not doubt that such a weapon would be needed because of the troubles they could expect to face on the long trail to the west.

'You know what will happen if you're wrong?' Tracey said seriously.

'We lose the wagons and most likely our lives into the bargain,' nodded the other. 'You won't have heard of me, but my name's Gideon Carter. You've ridden, as I have, some of those trails headin' west and you saw the same as I did, even before the War started. Prairies so wide that a man could ride for a month and not get to the other side, and river's so damned big and fast it's a hell job to ford 'em. And to top it all, a hundred men for every one we take with the wagons, men who've got the habits and viciousness of cougars. Ask anybody in town and they'll tell you we'll never got through. Too much against us along the way.'

'You know what I think?' Tracey spoke with a deadly seriousness. 'I think they're right when they say that. You'll never get through.'

'We've got to get through,' persisted the other harshly. 'This country is never going to grow until we can blaze a trail where a thousand, ten thousand men and women will follow us. There's a country out there on the Pacific, so big it could swallow all of these southern states.'

'That's a big gamble.'

'It's a gamble we've got to take. Like I said, I need a man who isn't afraid to face up to the kind of odds we'll meet along that trail. You'll consider the offer?'

'I will.'

'I'll be busy the rest of the day and tomorrow, getting in supplies and bringing all of the wagons together. But I'll be here again the following morning.'

'I'll let you know my answer then,' Tracey said quietly. He eyed the other as the man rose slowly to his feet, stood looking down at him for a long moment without speaking, then turned and made his way out of the dining-room. A moment later, Tracey glimpsed him crossing the dusty street outside, walking with a purposeful stride on to the shaded boardwalk on the opposite side of the wide street. He went into the store there, closing the door behind him.

Tracey leaned back in his chair, built a second smoke, something he had never done before. Pulling the smoke down into his lungs, he turned the other's offer over in his mind. There was no fear in his mind at the contemplation of moving all that way west. The other had not tried to belittle the dangers which could be expected all along the trail and clearly he had given a lot of thought into this business of moving a wagon trail across all those thousands of miles. A big undertaking; a hundred, perhaps two hundred days on the trail, facing wind and rain, burning sun and snow, mountains and plain, rivers and lakes, blazing a trail across a continent.

A tremendous undertaking, and did they have the weapons to make it? The Spencer was a good rifle, there was no denying that. It had come as a very unpleasant surprise to his own troop when they had first run up against these arms. But it was still in its first stages of design, they really needed a weapon more refined than that, and undoubtedly there would be one in time. But Gideon Carter did not look the sort of man who would wait until something like that happened. Already, he would be in the store, buying up the flour and beans they needed for this trip.

He finished his cigarette, then stood, stretching himself before going out into the warm sunlight and the drifting haze that lay low over the wide river and occasionally writhed along the streets near the waterfront. It was a strange place this town on the banks of the great Mississippi, a meeting place for every race and breed under the sun. French and Spanish, Negro and Indian, American, English and German, could all be found on these streets, a blend of turbulence and violence, sin and wickedness that could be matched in very few places in the South.

In the hot sunlight, the levee was still a riot of colour. A couple of small boats were tied up at the side of the quay, being unloaded, the negroes and the roustabouts wheeling cargo off the vessels and toting the fuel back, ready for them to leave and start the return trip as quickly as possible.

Tracey stood on the wooden boards, watching the activity. On the face of things, one would have thought that there was plenty of trade coming into these southern towns along this great river, that even after the war, things had soon come

right again for the defeated states. But nothing could have
been further from the truth. The Northern carpetbaggers
had moved in, were taking everything they could lay their
thieving hands on, leaving only the bare essentials for the
people who produced all of this wealth. There was a vast
market for southern beef and cotton, but it was being traded
for a few sacks of flour and beans. The South was starving
while it still had a million head of cattle with which to feed a
nation. Small wonder that more and more people were
moving out west, to get away from these restrictions, from all
of this poverty which had been forced on the states.

There was movement back along the streets and glancing over his shoulder, he saw the small bunch of wagons,
hauled by teams of strong horses, with one or two oxen
among them. Covered Conestoga wagons, he saw, sturdily
built, constructed of the strongest materials to last that
long journey west.

The wagons rolled to a standstill outside one of the livery
stables and men, women and children clambered down
into the dusty street. They would be gathering now if they
were to move out in a few day's time, he reflected, watching
the children playing around the wagons. If they survived
that journey to California, what sort of a country would they
grow up in? he wondered. Would they remember this day
when they told their grandchildren of how it was in the old
days just after the war, when they had pulled up stakes, piled
everything they had into a Conestoga wagon and moved
west in one of the greatest exoduses of all time?

Watching them, he already knew what his answer to
Gideon Carter would be. Maybe there was a chance they
would get through. It would be a fight, but there had to be
a trail out west, a trail blazed by men with gall and courage
and sweat. Hard men who moved west for profit and for
fun, who were willing to risk their lives to spread their
country across a continent. They would lose some men,
some women and children but sooner or later, they would
get the job done and he, Tracey Dillman, might have a
part in the shaping of it.

*

While Tracey Dillman was watching the wagons in the main street of New Orleans, more than two hundred miles to the west, there was activity of a different kind along the trail that wound across the frontier which divided the United States from the great wilderness that ran clear to the western coast of the country. It was cold that morning, with a drizzling rain that drove through the canebrake from clouds which were low and threatening. The scouts for the small train which had moved up from the east were riding back through the narrow valley between the towering bluffs that lifted in huge masses of red sandstone from the broad plains.

Laredo Clayton watched the trail for a moment and then looked to the east where the approaching wagon train ought to be. But there was no sign of anything yet, apart from the two riders, down below, walking their mounts back along the trail, their eyes wary, heads turning from side to side to take in everything, not once relaxing as they rode, even though they had scouted the trail on their way into the narrow valley and had obviously found nothing to alert them.

Carrico seated on a low rock a couple of feet away snorted in vague disgust. There was a thin, fixed smile on his craggy features and the vivid blue eyes that peered out from under the thick, bushy brows glittered viciously.

'I still figger it would have been simpler to take care of the scouts while we had the chance,' grunted Laredo harshly. 'Ain't much to fear from those men with the wagons, but those two down there will know how to fight and to shoot straight, we could've shot 'em both when they first rode into the valley.'

Carrico whirled on him, almost savagely. He said sourly. 'And give away the fact that we're here? They've got these scouts. That means they're expectin' trouble somewhere along the trail and this is where they'd be waitin' for it. Once those scouts report there's no sign of trouble, they'll come ridin' in and we can pick 'em off before they know we're here. You got the rest of the boys in position?'

Laredo nodded his head quickly. He glared angrily at the other. Someday, he told himself, Carrico would go too far, and he would have to slit his throat or put a bullet in him. But for the moment, they both needed each other and robbing and pillaging the wagon trains that came across this stretch of country was proving a little too profitable for him to consider breaking their association at the present time.

'Ride back along the ridge and keep an eye on the trail,' said the other after a brief pause, 'and don't let either of them two scouts spot you.'

Laredo got to his feet, still angry. But there was wisdom in the other's words and without saying anything further, he controlled his anger, moved into the canebrake and brought out his mount, swinging up into the saddle, wheeling the animal around, before moving away from the edge of the ledge, riding the big sorrel into the canebrake, crunching it underfoot. He felt cold and miserable, his wet clothing clinging to his body, chafing his flesh with every movement he made. The trail at this point led mostly through the cane and it caught at his legs, whipping against him from every side. Five minutes later, he was through the fringe of cane, and out of sight of anyone riding the valley trail. The horse knew this trail as well as he did, probably better, and he let it guide itself through the rocks. Most of the other men were crouched down closer to the trail and he knew, although he could not see or hear them, that they were just waiting for Carrico to give the signal.

Where the narrow trail swung down steeply, past upthrusting boulders and tall columns of wind-etched rock, he slid from the saddle, left the horse, and went forward on foot. From this vantage point, it was possible to look down and make out the two men, spurring their mounts now as they rode out of the valley, as if anxious to get back to the train. Lifting his head, Laredo narrowed his eyes against the grey light of the overcast heavens and just made out the wagons in the distance, five of them, he noticed, just as they had been warned to expect, battered Conestogas that crept slowly forward. They had paused to ford a wide stream about three miles away and now they had safely reached the nearer bank and were getting ready to push on into the valley which led through the deep hills and tall bluffs. Laredo ran a dry tongue over dry lips. Easy pickings, he thought tensely. Probably a couple of men to each wagon, plus the two scouts, making twelve men in all.

The scouts reached the wagon train, wheeled their mounts as they drew alongside it. Laredo thinned his lips in a vicious grin. Not much longer now, he thought inwardly. Once they rode on into the valley and Carrico judged they were in so far they didn't have any chance of turning and running back out again, he'd give the word. Laredo's right hand went down and fingered the long, flat-bladed knife at his waist, ran his thumb absently along the razor-sharp edge. There should be plenty of gold for the taking on the train, even though the wagons did seem to have been battered and driven hard along the trail. These folk brought everything they had with them when they made this trip because there could be no going back for any of them once they had left New Orleans and were headed west. They would have gold and supplies with them, possibly more guns. He pondered this as he seated himself on one of the smooth, flat stones beside the narrow trail. Carrico was different from him when it came to money. The other seemed to be more interested in the killing than he was in the gold these people carried. He liked to have money with him, but he was satisfied to take it as it came. Apparently he did not, like Laredo, consider what could be done with a few thousand dollars in gold. Then there would be no more need to live out here like an animal, or one of the Indians. He could move back east to one of the big cities, where he was not known, and every place would be open to him. He rubbed a hand over his chin, heard the stubble rasp under his flesh.

*

Saul Pattinson straightened on the tongue of the lead wagon, hands holding the reins tightly as he stared at the thickening cloud masses which lay over the tall bluffs directly ahead, then lowered his gaze to examine the narrow valley that ran between the towering columns of rock. They had moved through the narrow stream which had been less than a foot deep even in the middle, scarcely covering the stout wooden axles of the wheels. But once the rains, which had been threatening for a coluple of days now, came, there would be plenty of water in the rivers and streams and they might not find it so easy crossing the next stretch of water. His eyes dropped to the horses in the traces, watching the powerful, rhythmic motions of the muscles in their hindquarters as they strained with the heavy, creaking wagon. This had been the way of it for almost seventeen days since pulling out of New Orleans. There were in dangerous country now if the reports they had heard had been anywhere near the truth. The reports had told of armed bands of men lying in wait along the trails which led west. The Government had said they were unable to protect anyone moving west once they were outside of the towns. Along the trails, the final protection would have to come from themselves and he was a little worried, with only thirteen men in the train including the two scouts, they had little firepower if they were attacked, although the women could load and perhaps fire the guns if things got tough.

Another three miles or so and they would be driving into that valley. He would have preferred to drive around it but that would have added perhaps ten, maybe fifteen, miles to their journey and the country on either side looked arid and dry with probably no water for many miles. He watched the two scouts spurring their mounts back towards the train, kicking up the dust as the approached. A little sigh escaped from his lips. It was obvious from the way they rode, that they had seen nothing in the valley which indicated trouble. Not that this was a sure guarantee they would get through without trouble. If any of those armed bands was in the area, this was the logical place for an ambush.

The taller of the two scouts wheeled his mount, rode alongside the wagon. He called harshly: 'Ain't no sign of trouble ahead, Saul. Reckon it's clear to go through.'

'See any smoke?' asked Saul Pattinson.

'Nothin',' grunted the other. 'You still reckon there might be trouble yonder?'

'I don't know,' Pattinson sounded doubtful. He rubbed a hand over his chin. Teeth bit on his lower lip in thought, and his forehead was furrowed in taut concentration. 'We heard so many tales of outlaws in these parts and most of the folk we met at that last town reckoned that this *hombre* Carrico is operatin' in these parts. If that's right, then I figure he'll be somewhere close at hand.'

'What makes you so goshdarned sure?'

Pattinson smiled thinly. 'They'll know everythin' about us, maybe since we pulled out of New Orleans. They have spies everywhere passing the word along the line.' His words were positive things; not argumentative. 'I've heard of these men before, how they operate.'

'If any of 'em are in that valley yonder, we saw nothin' of them.' Perplexed, the other eased the long-barrelled rifle from its scabbard. He lifted his head, stared off into the distance through the thin drizzle of rain. Then he shook his head, a little wonderingly.

Pattinson leaned to one side in the wagon, peered back at the others following close behind, wheels creaking, horses straining ponderously in the traces, for this was rough uneven ground and he was anxious to get through that valley and into the grasslands which were said to lie beyond. Glancing up at the scout, he said tightly: 'Better ride back and warn the rest of the folk that we're going through the valley. Tell 'em to keep their hands close to their guns. We'll get precious little warnin' if we are attacked.'

As they drew closer to the narrow entrance of the valley, Pattinson's apprehension increased until he could scarcely control the tight fear in his mind. The rocky walls that hemmed in the trail rose sheer in many places, but here and there, he noticed, were other parts of the trail where the sandstone walls had tumbled down into a huddle of huge boulders and in these a dozen men could hide, ready to strike without warning. He sat tall and straight on the tongue of the wagon, lifted his gaze to probe the ragged crests where he guessed there might be another trail, a narrow animal track, hidden from where they were. If they had a look out posted up there, it might be possible to pick him out, with the sky at his back, although any man worth his salt would not make the mistake of silhouetting himself against the skyline. He saw nothing suspicious but this did nothing to allay the fear in his mind, the dread premonition that he could not still. Acting on impulse, he dragged the rifle from its position by his right boot, checked that it was loaded, placed it where it would be ready for use.

Time passed, slow, chilly and inexorable and in a little while, they rode into the deep stillness of the valley and the rocky walls lifted on either side of them so that they had the feeling of being shut off from all of the outside world, trapped within this stone tomb of a place where death might be hiding behind the next rock, the next boulder along the side of the trail.

Halfway along the valley now; still no sign of trouble. For a moment, Pattinson allowed himself to relax on the hard wood of the tongue. Maybe the scouts had been right, he reflected. They were both hardened veterans of the war and could be trusted. He still allowed his gaze to flick from one side of the trail to the other, but his mind was no longer as sharply alert as before and when the first shot did come, it came with the shocking suddenness of the unexpected.

The crisp bark of the rifle was still echoing along the high walls of the valley as the tall scout slumped sideways in his saddle, tried to hold life in the swiftly glazing eyes, then toppled to the rocky valley floor and lay still while the mount plunged on, leaping and neighing shrilly.

'Outlaws!' Pattinson got out the yelled warning, pulled up the ready loaded rifle, looked about him wildly for something at which to shoot. But he could see nothing. Then there was a brief flash among the boulders almost directly ahead of them, and the leaden smack of the bullet on the side of the wagon. He swung the rifle, sighted it on the spot where the flash had been, saw the head and shoulders of one of the outlaws appear for a second between two huge rocky and squeezed the trigger. The gun bucked hard against his wrists, but he felt a deep surge of satisfaction as he saw the man tumble out into the open, throwing up his hands high over his head as he fell headlong down the slope.

'Keep firing.' Raising his voice, Pattinson yelled as loudly as possible, but his words were caught up by the shattering echoes of gunfire flung back from the valley walls, but he stood up on the tongue of the wagon and waved his hand so that the others behind might see him. Savagely, he lashed at the horses in the traces, knowing that the only chance they had was to run the gauntlet of the outlaws' fire, get out of the valley before they could be trapped there. The old wagon creaked and groaned in all of its seams, the wheels bumped and spun on the rough ground. Clinging desperately to the reins as the horses threatened to run away with him, he drew the revolver from his waist, fired it at fleeting shadows that showed at intervals among the rocks. Behind him, the other men and some of the women were firing again. Shots came from high up on the narrow ledges that overlooked the trail. Madly, the horses pulled in the traces. The trail narrowed, wound away to the right, around a smooth curved bolder. Dropping the revolver, Pattinson hauled on the reins. Too late he saw that the outlaws had already blocked the trail. They must have watched for the scouts to ride back and report, and then rolled the rocks down from the upper reaches of the bluffs.

The horses swung wildly, terrified, away from the pile of rocks that lay against the foot of the cliff. The offside wheel struck, ripped with a cracking of wood and spun off. The wagon tilted crazily, threw him to one side. Then the Conestoga went down, slipping, twisting, lurching as the terrified horses continued to drag it along for several yards before they broke the leather of the traces and the team ran on, free at last. The long tongue of the wagon lay at right angles across the trail, blocking it for the others running up behind. There was no way past for them. Somehow, they were brought to a standstill before they too were piled up.

A savage yell came from somewhere among the rocks. 'Burn the canvas.'

The firing from the wagons was steady now and more accurate since they had come to a standstill. Another of the outlaws pitched forward, plummeting down from the rocks to crash within a few inches of the foremost wagon. Out of the corner of his eye, Saul Pattinson caught a glimpse of the dark, swarthy, bearded face, lips twisted into a grimace of hate, even in death. But the outlaws were still hunting cover, and coming forward, moving from one concealing shadow to another, firing as they came.

Two men leapt out from the boulders, raced towards the second wagon in the line, one man with flint and steel in his hands while the other dropped on one knee to cover him. It was evident what they intended, to fire the canvas and force out any of the occupants into the open where they could be cut down at leisure.

A rifle barked from the third wagon and the man with the flint fell over on to his back with a yell. He lay still and a few moments later, the man who had been with him scuttled back into the rocks, with bullets kicking up the dust at his heels. Then the blue-crimson lash of gunfire came from the rocks again and a hail of bullets poured into the trapped wagons. But worse was to come. Finding that there was little chance yet of getting close enough to the wagons to fire the canvas, the outlaws resorted to an old

Indian trick. Flaming brands fell on top of the wagons from the rocks overlooking the trail. Canvas began to burn. Smoke lifted in coils of grey into the still air. Still rifle shots came from the wagons although the fire had a firm hold now. But slowly, the overwhelming fire from the rocks was taking its toll.

Crouched down just inside the wagon, Pattinson continued to fire, loading and reloading with an icy calmness that seemed somehow out of place in his mind, now that the danger he had been dreading had finally materialized. A man came riding down one of the narrow gullies in the rocks, his horse stiff-legged as it slithered through the loose stones, sending them rattling down on to the trail ahead of it. Through the grey rain, Pattinson glimpsed a cruel face, saw the revolver lifted in the other's hand, the gun free and moving. There was the harsh stink of burnt powder in his nostrils, his vision was blurred by the tears that streamed from his eyes. The bullet caught him in the shoulder, slammed him back against the side of the wagon. Pain exploded inside him and it was his last ounce of strength that squeezed down on the trigger of the rifle. It kicked hard against the wounded shoulder, but he scarcely felt the pain. Through the haze that filmed his vision, he saw the man rear up in the saddle as he reined his mount directly in front of the smashed wagon. He seemed to be trying to stand on tiptoe, straining upward, an expression of shocked disbelief on his frozen features. Then he dropped his weapon, jack-knifed forward in the saddle, fingers slipping from the reins, curling forward to drop solidly into the dirt.

Carrico rode slowly towards the wagons. He had watched from a distance, determined not to expose himself to any of the rifle fire which he had noticed had been accurate. Seven of his men had been killed, far more than he had expected. In the middle of the trail, all of the wagons were burning fiercely, but some of the men, ignoring the flames, were crawling under them, searching for the gold which would be hidden there.

When they had searched every wagon, made sure that no one was still alive, he sat waiting for them. 'Well?' he asked tightly, as Laredo rode up. 'What did they get?'

'Five bags. We haven't opened them yet. Some whiskey and supplies, though most of that got burned.'

'We can get plenty of supplies,' grunted Carrico. He let his cold, cruel gaze run over the bodies of the men and women. His eyes were gleaming viciously.

The leather bags were brought forward and handed to Carrico who weighed them in his hands, assessing the amount of gold they each contained.

He grinned savagely. 'A good day's work,' he said finally. He looked up quickly at the sound of moaning from one of the wagons. Swiftly, he jerked his hand towards one of the men. The other went forward, plucked the knife from his belt as he did so, vanished around the side of the wagon. A moment later, the low moaning stopped and the man came back, wiping the blade on his shirt. Carrico nodded slightly.

'What do we do with the bodies?' asked Laredo harshly. He eyed Carrico speculatively.

'Leave them here,' said the other roughly. 'The buzzards will get 'em without us botherin' about 'em.' He hefted the leather bags on to the saddle of his mount, then swung up quickly.

Laredo's sharp eyes continued to watch him closely. 'When you goin' to count out that money?' he asked tautly.

'You'll get your share,' retorted the other. He swung his horse about and rode off along the trail.

Laredo watched him with a thin, cynical smile on his lips. His own time would come soon, he told himself tightly. Carrico would not be running this outfit for much longer. He did not underestimate the other's ruthlessness or cunning, and he doubted if he was as fast as Carrico on the draw, but if he got the other before he was aware there was any trouble, things could be turned to his advantage. He'd had it in mind to ask Carrico to divide the spoils there and then and that would give him time to ride back into one of the small towns of this territory where he would be a big man with all of that money. The thought fanned a fire in his brain, a flame he found difficult to control.

Leaping up into the saddle, he rode out of the valley, past the body of the man who had been shot down by Pattinson's final despairing act. He scarcely gave the slain man a second glance. The men who joined this band knew what to expect sooner or later. It would not be long before the wagon trains would be given escorts, perhaps of cavalry, to take them unhindered through this stretch of territory. When that happened, they would either have to give up this business, or move on further west, ready to attack once the Army escorts left the trains and returned east to accompany some other one west.

An hour later, after riding through the swampland which bounded the wide river, they worked their way up to higher ground, into the rolling hills, covered with the green patches of woods. The lakes and the river were stagnant and the mist that was perpetually there mingled and blended with the drizzle, making the air heavy.

Then, as they rode on to higher ground, the fog lifted, Laredo breathed more easily and gave his mount its head as they entered thick brush which would have proved impassable even to a horse had there not been a narrow, twisting path which led back to the upper reaches of the river. Here, the cane had been levelled and in the clearing thus formed, the small cluster of wooden shacks had been built, with the cane thrown haphazardly over roofs and walls so that they could easily be missed even from close to. They dismounted, letting the horses go loose. They would not stray too far from the clearing. Not only was the cane thick all around, but there were the swamps near the river.

Lowering his head, while the rest of the men went to their respective huts, Laredo ducked inside the largest shack. In the dark, gloomy interior, he saw Carrico standing with his legs braced well apart. The leather bags were placed in a neat pile in the middle of the floor. Then Laredo saw that the other was not alone. There was someone else standing in the shadows near the rear of the hut. He let his gaze flick swiftly and appraisingly to the other, then relaxed as he recognized one of the Mexican halfbreeds from New Orleans.

'Miguel was here when I arrived,' Carrico said evenly. 'Before we start dividin' the gold, I figure we'd better hear what he has to say.'

Laredo shrugged, squatted on the side near the gold. His eyes never once left the other's face.

'There is big wagon train in New Orleans waiting to pull out,' said the other thinly. 'They head in this direction, I am sure.'

'How many wagons?' asked Laredo. He turned his gaze from Carrico and studied the half-breed deliberately.

'A dozen, maybe more by now. They were coming in while I was there. A man called Carter is leading them. They have much silver and gold to buy land in California.'

'California!' Laredo stared back into the black, sloe eyes. 'You sure they ain't got an escort with 'em for a trip like that?'

'No, *señor*.' The half-breed shook his head. 'I am sure. But I did hear that Señor Carter was trying to get men to ride with him, men who had fought in the war and knew how to handle guns. They also have rifles you do not need to load after every shot.'

'Spencer rifles,' muttered Carrico. 'I saw them during the war with the Union forces.' He spat into the dirt of the floor. 'They are not to be trusted for all they claim for them. Give me a rifle like this every time against one of them.' He picked up the rifle which lay against the wall of the hut in one corner.

Laredo did not seem to notice. He said thickly. 'How much money you think they have?'

'Much gold and silver. Seventy, eighty thousand dollars.'

Carrico said tersely: 'They should reach here in fifteen

maybe sixteen days after pulling out from New Orleans. That means we can expect 'em ten days from now.' He swung on the half-breed. 'You left town six days ago?'

'*Si*, Senor Carrico.' The Mexican nodded. 'Six days.'

'Then we won't bother any of the immigrants movin' through until that train arrives. We can't be sure of killin' them all as we did that train in the valley and I don't want stories to get back to this other wagon train until it comes through.'

'You sending out scouts to watch for this train?' asked Laredo.

'Time enough for that,' Carrico growled. He picked up the stone jug of liquor from the floor, hooked his fingers through the handle and lifted it high along the back of his arm, drinking noisily from the neck, some of the liquid spilling over and running down his neck and on to his bare chest where the shirt was open. He looked up at the half-breed. 'Better stay here until we need you again. There's plenty of room now. We lost some men attacking that last train.' His tone hardened. 'They fight more fiercely now. Soon we won't be able to stop them and if the Army decides to move up with them and set up fortified posts along the trail, things will get more difficult.'

'There was talk of that in New Orleans,' muttered Miguel. He took the jug which the other held out to him, drank deeply for a moment, then wiped a hand over his lips. 'The settlers are complainin' that the Government is doin' nothing to protect 'em. Soon, they will send soldiers with them.'

TWO

Death Lies Waiting

Tracey Dillman checked his mount on a rise of ground that looked out over the broad lands which stretched away on the far side of the wide, sluggish river, leading out to the flat desert which lay beyond. Behind him were the wagons, fifteen in all, lumbering slowly forward, axles groaning under the tremendous weight of furniture and provisions which were carried in them, rocking and swaying from side to side as the horses and oxen strained to haul them up the rising stretch of ground.

A lean, hatchet-faced man sat his horse beside Tracey, swaying a little in his saddle from weariness. The heat head pressed down on the plains like the flat of a mighty, crushing hand and overhead, the sun was a bright disc of fire in the cloudless heavens, glaring harshly off the ground, shocking back from the rocks with a dizzying light. Denton lifted an arm and pointed across the river.

'Those are the flats,' he said in a dull monotone. 'We've been travellin' fast since we left Twin Creeks, but that stretch will slow us down plenty.'

Tracey nodded. The alkali was an almost blinding white sheet that lay spread out beyond the river almost as far as the eye could see until it hazed gradually in the far distance into low, undulating hills across the horizon.

'We'll get the wagons over and then rest up for a spell,

26

at least until the heat's down a bit.' He turned in the saddle, signalled with one hand. The wagons rumbled forward slowly, wheels turning on greased axles, trundling towards the top of the rise from where they would run down the gentle slope to the river. He could make out Gideon Carter seated on the tongue of the lead wagon, hands holding the reins efficiently and easily, guiding the four horses as they tugged and strained, feet pawing at the ground as they put all of their weight and strength into their task. They topped the rise, swung down to the river. Tracey cast about him warily for a long moment, before riding down to join them. The country here was flat and stiff, with few places for a man to hide and he felt reasonably confident they would encounter no trouble until they had crossed that stretch of alkali and were on the other side. Stories had filtered back to New Orleans about the outlaw bands that roamed this wild and untamed territory. They spoke of men such as Carrico and Laredo, leaders of ruthless cut-throat killers who had, if the stories were to be believed, stopped and robbed more than a dozen trains in the past few years, killing every man, woman and child on board so that there would be no witnesses to talk against them.

'We'll get 'em across the river and then make camp until later in the day,' he said, riding up to the lead wagon.

Carter gave a brief nod. He had long since known better than to argue with this steely-eyed man who seemed used to giving commands rather than taking them. He knew little about the other, except that the colour of his cloth when he had met him in New Orleans had been grey, that he had fought on the losing side during the war. Maybe, he reflected, as he put his horses to the water, there was still a bitterness in the other's mind. Certainly he would have seen many things which altered a man, scarred him inwardly for life, no matter how hard he tried to forget such events. War changed men in many subtle ways.

The river was slow-moving, shallow, even in the middle where it ran thick and muddy. There had been the rains of a few days back, but they had brought little rise to the waters here and there was no difficulty in getting the heavily laden wagons across. The scouts swam their mounts a little further upstream, checked the far bank for tracks and found none that were recent.

On the far bank, although they could see no real reason for it, the wagons were formed into their inevitable circle and everyone settled down to try to find some shade from the fierce sun. It was not easy. Even inside the wagons themselves, with the air hot and unmoving, there was no respite from it. The tattered canvas caught the heat and held it in until every breath was like a blast of air from some terrible oven, burning chest and lungs and bringing no refreshment to tired bodies.

Tracey lay under one of the wagons, feeling the heat from the ground soak up into his back. Sweat stood out on his face and body until his shirt stuck to his flesh, chafing and irritating whenever he moved. With the down sun, there was little change. The heat still remained and the ground shimmered around them, the air filled with the scent of burnt grass and hot alkali. The horses drooped in the traces, heads lowered, grounded by the reins, feeling the heat like the others.

Until the sun was almost on the horizon during the evening, they made no move at all. Then they got the wagons ready, and moved out on to the trail that was just visible across the alkali. They rode with the red glare of the sun shining directly in their eyes, rode with the rising dust of the desert in their nostrils, and even though they had their kerchiefs over their nostrils, it soon worked its way into their noses and mouths, going down their throats and into their lungs, burning and choking.

Soon, a cooling wind blew down from the mountains in the far distance, but the dust was still there, churned up by the hooves of the horses and oxen. The ground was soft here and wheels sank deep into it, adding to the difficulties they had. They made slow progress as Denton had prophesied. Travelling during the early part of the night with the white face of the moon lifting from the eastern horizon and throwing an eerie, ghostly light over the stretching desert, they drove steadily westward until the moon had lifted to its zenith when Tracey called a halt. Tracey picketed the horse, hobbled the night horses and turned most of the others out to graze on what little grass they could find in that terrible country. After that, he helped the cook with the camp chores. The women got the food ready and a fire was built in the open space between the wagons. Guards were posted to keep watch through the night although there seemed little chance of any attack here. The ground was too open for any one to get close enough to the wagons without being seen although there might be danger from marauding bands of renegade Indians.

Rolling into his blankets, an hour later, he fell asleep almost at once. There was the burning itch of alkali on his skin under the clothes, and it had formed into a mask on his face, but they had little water with them to spare for washing and it was a discomfort most of them would have to put up with until they reached the far side of the flats.

Before the first pale light of dawn flooded the scene, while the moon was still clearly visible close to the western horizon now, they were on the move again, grumbling a little at this early start, but recognizing that if they were to make the other side of the alkali flats before their water ran out, they had no other choice. To drive on through the heat of the middle of the day was plain suicide on both the animals and themselves. Daybreak found them well on the trail. Three miles, five miles. The wagons jostled and swayed dangerously and there were the usual incidents which had to be met and overcome. A wagon caught and stuck in the dust, wheels bogged down to the axles, horses straining vainly in the traces. There there was nothing for it but to get everyone out and put their own weight against it, heaving and thrusting cursing and sweating, until the wheels finally broke free and the horses were able to take the strain once more and keep the Conestoga moving. A lot of the wagons were too heavily loaded for safety. But the women had refused to leave New Orleans without the items of furniture which they had brought with them from way back east. It had been useless to try to point out to them that there, the trails between the big towns had been broad strips of hard land running through lush green country. Out here, there were often no trails at all and once a wagon was stuck it meant holding up the rest of the train until they succeeded in pulling it free.

Tracey talked it over with Gideon Carter when they were on the move again. 'Pretty soon, we're goin' to have to make some of them women see sense and get rid of some of their loads,' he said tersely. 'We've had to stop three times this mornin' to pull one or other of the wagons free. Once we get into that country where these outlaw bands are reckoned to be operatin' we won't have time for that and these folk have got to be made to see that their lives are far more important than these bits of furnuiture they insist on carryin'. They'll be able to get more once we hit California. If we ever get there,' he added significantly.

'You still worryin' about those outlaws we heard about?' queried the other. He leaned back in the wagon, pulled out a tobacco pouch which had been hanging just inside the opening and held it out to Tracey. The other took it with a muttered word of thanks, rolled himself a smoke, then handed the pouch back to the other. He drew the smoke gratefully into his lungs. It soothed the itching in his throat a little and allowed him to think things out a little more clearly than before.

'Sure I'm worried,' he nodded, staring out through slitted eyes across the glaring plain that stretched away in front of them. 'Just because we've seen nothin' so far, don't allay my fears at all.'

'I figure we've got enough men to hold 'em off if they do decide to attack,' said the other confidently. He clucked the reins over the backs of the horses. For a moment, they increased their gait, then just as quickly, fell back into their original slow rhythmic movement. 'And with these rifles, we ought to beat them.'

'I hope you're right.' Tracey did not feel as confident as the other. The border gangs were organised, had their spies everywhere, knew the movements of the wagon trains since they left New Orleans or Natchez.

They drove on, well into the day, until the terrible burning heat forced them to halt again. Sunlight hard on white alkali; a vast, shining, eye-searing stretch of dry ground which lay interminably ahead of them, broad and parched, devoid of water, uncrossed by rivers and the few streams which had once crossed it were not little more than faintly visible channels in the white dust, cracked and caked where all of the moisture, down to the very last drop, had long since been sucked from the earth by the avid heat of the sun. This was a death valley between the hills to the east and the higher range of mountains which lay almost directly to the west. Someday, it would be the state of Oklahoma, but not yet, not with only the few, scattered wagon trains moving through on their way west, with few towns and only a handful of military posts dotted here and there, more to keep the Indian nations at bay than to protect the immigrants from their own kind.

Two days later, they moved out of the alkali flats into greener, more lush territory that bordered the foothills of the mountains. Here, there was danger of a kind different from that which they had faced during the past three days. Then it had been death from hunger and thirst, from the blistering sun; here it was death, quick and sudden from the bullet of a hidden marksman. Less than five miles ahead, the ground levelled off and there was a broad river running across the trail and beyond it, tall bluffs with a narrow valley which meandered between the rising walls of a steep canyon. He eyed it contemplatively as he sat his mount on a small knoll. These were the places a man came to look upon for danger. He would have perhaps thought it best for them to swing north at this point, move along the eastern bank of the river, maybe fording it ten miles or so further upstream, then crossed more open country, but that would add many miles to their journey

and he doubted if the others would listen to him should
he suggest it. It was only a hunch he had that there was
trouble lying in wait for them in that narrow valley beyond
the river, the feeling a man who had been through the war
tended never to ignore. He knew he could not explain a
feeling such as this to men like Carter. Only Denton might
understand, an old cavalry man himself. He turned his
mount, rode back to where the wagons were rumbling
slowly westward.

With a tremendous effort of will, he forced the feeling
away, thrust it from him. They had to go on now, there
could be no turning back, but if they were all forewarned
of the possibility of trouble, were not taken by surprise,
there was a chance they could fight their way through if
there was any trouble. He rode up to the lead wagon, held
up his hand. Carter reined in the sweating, lathered
horses, tied off the reins.

'Trouble?' he asked quietly, though with a little of the
steel showing through his voice. His eyes flickered ahead
of them, across to the river, and then beyond, lips pressed
into a tight, hard line.

'Mebbe,' Tracey gave a quick, short nod. 'Looks too
good a place for an ambush in that valley yonder between
the bluffs for anybody watching for a wagon train to miss.
My guess is that if we do run into one of these gangs, that's
where they'll hit us. Better warn everybody to be ready for
trouble once we cross that river.'

'We could make a detour round this place,' suggested
the other after a long, reflective pause.

Tracey shook his head. 'Too far. It would add fifteen
miles or more. And we ain't no way of tellin' whether there
mightn't be more waiting to the north.'

'Then we go through,' said the other determinedly.
'We'll water the horses and fill the barrels at the river, then
push on. We ought to get well through that pass before
nightfall and there's probably more open ground on the
other side with grass for the livestock.'

Although running sluggishly, the river was high. Here,

it had clearly caught the full weight of the recent rains higher in the mountains and the muddy water, brownish-red, rolled heavily between its banks where in some places, they had caved in, the water catching at the mud and taking it along with it, tearing large gaps in the earth. Now and then, however. a piece of wood or brush would move past them in the middle of the river, turning over and over, giving them an indication of just how strong, how power-ful, the current really was out there, and how deeply the water had gouged that central channel out of the river bed.

Tracey Dillman looked at the rushing limbs of brush and then around him at the tall brush which, in places, grew right down to the water's edge, tufts of tall, wiry grass that shone a little in the early afternoon sunlight. Finally, he twisted in the saddle, motioned to Carter, watched as the other applied the whip to the horses and brought the wagon to the river bank. The wagons were strung out now, meandering slowly in the direction of the river, as though they had all the time in the world in which to reach it, and their drivers were content to accept the chance that there was no likelihood of trouble here. They had all been warned that they might run into an ambush once they hit the valley some three miles away and their rifles, all of the repeating Spencer variety, were ready and loaded.

Under the huge emptiness of the sky which stretched in a vast inverted bowl of blue over their heads, unsullied by clouds, the wagons waited. The horses were covered with a haze of dust that had clung to their coats during the long, cruel drive across the flats. They had smelled water, as had the cattle, trailing along behind the wagons, teth-ered by ropes to the rear wheels. Now they gave vent to bull-throated roars, pawing at the ground impatiently.

'You figure we ought to put 'em straight in?' asked Carter, nodding towards the river. 'Looks higher than we reckoned.'

Tracey shook his head. 'They're a mite pernickety, getting to the water after that haul across the alkali. Soon

as you get your wagon over, we'll put the rest in. Once they
have a lead we shouldn't get much trouble. May have to
swim the horses over though. Reckon too, we'd better get
some raitas tied to the back to hold the wagon when it
starts floating or you'll go clear to the Gulf.'

Carter waited until three of the other men had fastened
their ropes to the back of the wagon, checking that the
knots were secure, then he kicked off the thick wooden
brake, sent it forward, rolling down the gentle slope, with
the horses pulling hard. At the river's edge, they baulked,
caught the surge of the current. Savagely, Carter yelled at
them, used the whip on their backs, sent them forward
into the swirling water. For a long moment, the horses
jostled each other sideways, then they went in, plunged for
a moment, rearing as the water hit their chests, bucking
the current. Savagely, Carter hauled on the reins as the
wagon began to lift. Floating helplessly for a moment it
began to drift, then steadied as he managed to turn the
horses upstream. The current swirled around the sides of
the Conestoga and there were moments when it tilted
crazily, threatening to topple over out of control, but
always it righted itself miraculously as the ropes behind
tautened, were hauled straight, holding it on course. Once
they had helped Carter past the middle of the river, the
men had to cast off their ropes or be dragged in after him.
Already, the riatas were at their fullest stretch. The
covered wagon drifted on the current for several yards
until the team got their footing on the river bed, struggled
up the further bank, dragging the wagon behind them.
Tensed and excited, Tracey watched as it moved up the
bank, out of the shallows, with water dripping from its
underside, spilling out of the interior where some had
washed on board.

One by one, the rest of the wagons were put into the
river and edged across. The ochre coloured water,
running high with mud, tore at them, tried to pull them
downstream as if angry at not taking any of them along on
the deep, strong current. Then Tracey put his own mount

into the stream. The dingy water swirled about him, tugged at his legs in the saddle, washed coldly against him. The horse whiskered and snorted, then breasted the current and struck out for the opposite bank. Once he was on dry ground again, there was time to check on any casualties there had been. A wheel spinning slowly loose from the last wagon to go over and three of the steers they had brought with them had been lost, caught by the vicious, cunning river and whirled far to the south. But they had been lucky, there was no doubt about that. A river in flood was a bad thing and had taken the lives of many men.

By now, the sun was lowering to the west, slipping down the wide arch of the sky. There was no time to wait and dry out. They had to be through that valley before dark and as far as possible on the other side. Tracey rode ahead with Denton, scouting the land, eyes wary and alert. Everything was quiet here, with nothing moving and no sound to disturb the stillness. Only an occasional buzzard could be seen, a whirling tattered piece of black cloth against the blue of the sky.

'Nothin' here,' muttered Denton harshly. He pulled a wad of tobacco from his saddle pouch, thrust it between strong teeth and wrenched a piece off with a twist of his neck muscles, chewing thoughtfully on it.

'I ain't too sure,' grunted Tracey. He let his glance drift slowly along the topmost ledges of the rocks that crowded down on the trail at this point. There was a quietness here that he did not like. They rode on into the valley and all the time, he had that itchy feeling between his shoulder blades, as if he was being watched all of the way, but whenever he turned sharply in the saddle and glanced about him, he saw nothing suspicious. In the end, Denton gave a harsh laugh.

'You're gettin' too jumpy,' he said. 'There's nobody here, been nobody for quite a spell.'

'There's no way of tellin' that,' Tracey retorted. 'The rains have washed the trail clean of tracks.' They rode around a smooth outcrop of rock which thrust its way into the trail at this point, bending it sharply. Riding around the rock, he reined his mount sharply, caught at the other's bridle.

For a moment, they sat there, each man conscious of one single thought: *That Denton had been wrong, and that somebody had been there, quite recently.*

Denton sucked in a sharp breath. 'I guess you were right,' he said thickly. He stepped down from his horse and went forward slowly until he stood beside the nearest wagon. The canvas had been burnt and now lay in black ashes on the blistered paintwork and the singed wooden struts. One of the wheels lay off its axle. The horses had obviously broken loose shortly after the catastrophe which had befallen the small wagon train, or more probably had been taken by the outlaws. There were evidently several indications that the train had been looted and no sign of fire arrows, showing that it had not been an Indian raid. The outlaws had hurled flaming fire-brands down on the wagons from the rocks over the trail and had shot the defenders when they were forced out into the open by the fire.

Tracey felt sickened by what he saw, the wanton killing of everyone on board the train, the utter destruction that had been wrought here by men who obviously had no regard for human life. He forced the sickness away, felt the deep-seated anger rising in him. There was nothing they could do here. The train had been attacked and wiped out over a week, maybe ten or fifteen days before.

'Reckon we'd better warn the others,' said Denton thinly. His stare was a dull thing as he looked across at Tracey in the dull gloom, where the rocks shut out every vestige of sunlight. His face was a pale grey under the leathery tan.

'I reckon so,' Tracey nodded. 'But we'll still have to come through.'

'Past this,' said Denton harshly. He jerked a thumb in the direction of the smashed and burnt wagons that littered the trail.

'We'll have to. There's no other way and we'd be caught just as they were if we make camp out yonder this side of the river.'

There was no answer from the other. The expression on his face told Tracey that Denton realized just how true this was. They had committed themselves this far and they had to go on now. He realized that he had been thinking that the men who had done this were still around. The truth was probably that they were in another state by now, hundreds of miles from here.

As they rode back, they kept their eyes open, left the main trail and rode up into the rocks where a narrow, twisting trail wound around the face of the tall bluffs. Rocks moved treacherously underfoot and in places they were forced to dismount and walk with their horses, shuffling forward, one behind the other. The trail led them over the brow of the hills, down into the valley where the wagon train stood waiting. They had seen nothing among the rocks, but there was still that *feeling* which they could not throw off. Saddling up, they rode the rest of the way, wheeling their mounts.

'Find anythin'?' called Carter. He stood up on the tongue of the wagon, a stocky figure with the red sunlight falling full on his bluff features.

'Sure did,' Denton yelled back. 'Wagon train in that valley yonder. Must've been ambushed by outlaws maybe a coupla weeks ago. Everybody killed, wagons fired and no sign of the horses.'

Tracey saw Carter's face tighten at the news, heard the faint murmurs of conversation from the other wagons as the news spread, saw the frightened looks on the faces of the women, the way the men pulled their rifles closer to them, fingers tightening on the reins as they sat taut in the wagons.

Carter's voice was cold and still as he said tensely: 'What do we do then? Ride on and take the risk or stay here for the night and then move back in the morning, try to work our way around here?'

'That won't solve anythin',' Tracey told him tightly. 'We have to move on through that valley now. But I figure we stand a good chance. Ain't likely that they'll stick around once they pull a job like that. Too scared of a possee moving out from one of the towns nearby or getting the Army on their trail.'

'And if they are there?' posed the other.

'Then we'll fight. At least they won't take us by surprise as they did that other train.'

Carter nodded. Standing tall on the tongue of the wagon, he gave the signal for those behind him to move forward. Every man in that train knew what to expect. The guns were loaded and the women were under the cover of the canvas ready to fire too if they had to. Slowly, ponderously, creaking in every axle and seam, the wagons rumbled towards the rising bluffs that thrust their tremendous walls of red sandstone up from the flat plain.

Sometimes, when a man had lived close to the land all his life, when he has seen death come close without actually touching him personally, he gets into the growing habit of knowing what is going to happen that split second before it actually does. This had happened to Tracey Dillman several times in the past and was one on the reasons he was still alive. Now, riding alongside one of the wagons as they drove forward, he was uncommonly bothered by the feeling that all of this, all of what lay ahead of him was not going to come out right for him or the others in the train.

He gigged his mount as the sense of uneasiness grew swiftly, rode up to the front of the column. The trail was a solid streak of dust that wound away in front of them, occasionally vanishing out of sight whenever it twisted and turned sharply through the rocks. Halfway along the canyon, he brought down his spurs, suddenly certain that trouble was ready to break, in spite of the fact that he and Denton had seen nothing when they had ridden that higher trail half an hour before. He got the unshakeable impression of men cross-crossing the upper trails, moving into position and above the rumble of the wagons themselves, he thought he caught the tag ends of sound as they worked their way forward with their urgent hastes. He was in a notch of the canyon, with the wagons some little distance behind, just out of sight, the high rough walls holding him strictly to the trail, when he heard the first volley of shots that rattled down from the tall rocks. The firing stayed brisk, not heavy volleys, but a steady rattle of sound that sent him leaping from the saddle, pulling the rifle from its scabbard. Gripping it tightly in both hands, he ran back along the dusty trail. Ahead of him, a ragged burst of shots rang out, the disembodied echoes chasing each other along the canyon. He looked anxiously to the shadowed bank on either side and knew that he could not climb off the trail at this point. Nor had he time to go back for the horse, in the hope that it might be able to get up into the rocks. The outlaw band was a vague motion on either side of the wagon train. He shoved himself flat against the side of the rocks, whipped up the rifle and fired a couple of shots into the rocks, aiming at the far side of the canyon. Even though it was a repeater rifle, there was the need to cock the hammer with every shot and this slowed the firing to half of what it might have been had the action been fully automatic.

He heard a man cry out almost directly in front of him: 'I've been hit! I can't make it.'

Risking a quick glance, he saw Carter slump in his seat, hands clawing for a gun at his waist. Obviously he had emptied the magazine of the Spencer and had been reaching for his revolver when the bullet had caught him, pitching him backward into the wagon. The marksmen on the rim of the hills pumped their shots with a methodical thoroughness down into the train, bullets crashing through the thin canvas. From within the wagons came the shrill screams of wounded women and children. Tracey veered in until he was crouching low in the rocks. He could just see Denton's lanky form on the far side, aiming and firing whenever a head appeared among the rocks.

Lifting his glance, he made out the dark head and shoulders of one of the outlaws high up near the rim of the bluffs. Crouching down, steadying himself against an upthrusting rock, he brought the man's head into the notch of his sights, took up the slack of the trigger, then squeezed it tightly. At first, he thought he had missed, then he saw the man roll forward, drop several feet until his body was tightly wedged in a natural cleft among the rocks. Circling great masses of fallen rock and soil, he fought his way forward over some of the roughest footing he had ever encountered. There was no point in trying to reach the wagons. It would be sheer suicide to try to cross the intervening open ground. He would be picked off long before he had reached cover. Better to remain here on the very edge of the trail, where he could find plenty of cover and pick off any of the outlaws foolish enough to show themselves. They seemed to be getting a mite careless now, showing their heads over the rocks whenever they fired at the wagons. A steady fire continued to come from inside the canvas covers of the Conestogas, forcing the outlaws to keep their distance. The Spencer rifles were giving the immigrants an advantage but it was not as great a one as they had hoped; and the slight edge which the semi-automatic fire gave them was offset by the greater numbers of the outlaws who were well hidden among the rocks overlooking the trail at this point. They had chosen an excellent place for an ambush, where the trail wound around a sharp bend, narrowing until it was only just possible to get a wagon through.

More bullets crashed into the wagons. Some whined in shrieking ricochet off the metal struts and braces, others simply went through the canvas with a rough tearing impact and as often as not, struck flesh and bone without warning. He had a creepy feeling about this, as if he had experienced it all before. The sound brought back the smells of the war, the thick, acrid stench of powder in his nostrils, the harsh whinneying of the frightened horses struggling frantically in the leather traces as they fought to free themselves. One of the wagons, out of control, began to run forward as the horses hauled on it. Tracey had a brief glimpse of the driver slumped forward on the tongue of the wagon as it careered from side to side, crashing against the rough rocks which tore at the canvas but helped to keep the wagon upright, veering crazily from one side of the trail to the other, just missing Carter's wagon, then coming on, straight for Tracey. The driver was either dead or badly wounded, unable to hold the plunging horses as they carried the wagon forward. A woman appeared in the opening between the tattered strips of canvas, tried to brace herself and move forward to grab the reins from her husband. Almost, she reached them. Then one of the wheels struck an upthrusting stone in the trail, crunched into shattered ruin, fell to pieces under the smashing impact. The wagon lurched, then lifted high into the air, hung there for one incredible second as though suspended by strings before turning over and crashing down with a roar that shook the ground and grated on Tracey's ears. Before his stunned gaze the woman was thrown from the wagon and hurled into the rocks where she fell and lay still, unmoving. A small moment of panic made him jerk and roll away. Shots were coming from the rocky ledges now, aimed carefully and deliberately at anything that moved. Tracey crawled further along the edge of the trail. From the way that woman had gone done after hitting the rocks, he knew there was nothing he nor anyone else could do for her. The firing swung round. It seemed to be directed more at him now than the wagons, smashing into the rocks, hammering off the hard, dusty ground of the trail, lifting little spurts of the grey muck wherever a bullet struck. The fire was a terrible thing and he knew that all of them had underestimated the full strength of these organized bands of outlaws. It was a savage destruction that shook him to his very core.

He had come under fire such as this before, during the bitter battles that had culminated in Appomatox, but then there had been other men, trained soldiers, to back him up. Now there seemed to be no one. Denton had stopped firing and through the haze of dust that lifted over the scene he saw the other slumped back, spread-eagled against one of the rocks, his face upturned to the sky, eyes staring wide, but seeing nothing. He lay flat, not so much frightened by the noise as awed by the flailing destruction of it. He had made a big mistake in leading the train into the valley, in trusting to the Spencer rifles to turn the trick for them and in his vague belief that maybe the outlaws would not be anywhere close to the spot where they had destroyed that other train only a little while before. Every single muscle in him was so tight that it ached to move his body; and there were the biting fingers of cramp in the knotted muscles of his legs. His mind however, was very clear and sharp, magnifying all of the sounds around him, picking out the faint scrape of boots on the rocks at his back a split second before the man appeared around one of the huge round boulders less than ten feet above the trail. Tracey spun on his heels, threw himself backward, felt his shoulders strike the sharp-edged rocks under him, but his gun was in his right hand, finger squeezing down on the trigger even as the bearded outlaw tried to bring his own weapon to bear.

The bullet took the other full in the chest, kicking him back a little on his heels. Tracey clearly saw the dust lift from the man's shirt, then saw the red stain of blood there as he dropped his gun clattering on to the rocks at his feet and pitched forward, an expression of shocked disbelief frozen on to his face. He struck the rocks a little above where Tracey lay, rolled and toppled down to crash on to the valley floor a few feet away. His body lay slackly in death and Tracey turned back to face the rest of the men who came yelling down the side of the valley now that the volume of fire from the wagons had slackened appreciably.

One palm came down on the end of a needle-shaped rock, the onthrusting weight of his shoulders pushing it deep into his flesh. Gritting his teeth together, he pulled out the sliver of rock. Blood gushed into his palm but he ignored it and in that same moment, there was the bark of a gun close by, but he never heard it for something took him on the side of the head, knocked him sprawling into the rocks.

THREE

Trail of Fury

When he finally came round, his head was aching with a fierce hammering agony that sent stabs of pain lancing into his brain. For a long moment, he lay in the utter darkness, feeling the chill coldness of his body, soaking into his limbs, as he tried to recall what had happened, how he came to be there. He blinked his eyes several times, then saw that it was not quite dark, that there was a faint light of some kind by which he could just make out the high, rocky walls that loomed over him. Beyond them, he made out the faint glimmer of starlight and memory came back with a rush. He forced himself up into a sitting position and almost at once sank back down again as the rocks and starlit sky whirled sickeningly around him and a wave of dizziness swept over him.

Fumbling, he managed to push himself on to his elbows again and this time, with a tremendous effort of will, forced down the agony, kept his eyes open in spite of the red flashes that darted in front of his vision. Shock made him almost reel. Around him lay the splintered remains of the wagons which had been ambushed. No one moved in the dark shapes. Groaning a little, he got to his feet, stood swaying for a long moment, one hand resting on the cold rocks for support which was so necessary. Putting up his other hand to his head, he felt the crustiness of congealed

44

blood on the side of his temple, winced as pain shot through him at the touch. A slug had struck him on the side of the head, knocking him cold, and yet was the means of saving his life. The outlaws had taken him for dead, leaving him where he lay. The body of the man he had shot still lay a few feet away, untouched.

Gradually, his senses returned and he contrived to remain on his feet, releasing his hold on the rocks and staggering forward, the throbbing in his head making it difficult for him to think properly. The bullet had clearly just creased his skull, knocking him unconscious, glancing off the bone, but not doing any more serious damage. The valley spun around him in a dizzying spiral and he sucked in a deep breath, waiting for the scene to hold still, then risked a few more steps forward. Gradually, he was able to distinguish the wagons, some of them overturned where they had struck the sides of the canyon, others still upright with the horses standing in the traces, clustered together as if finding safety in numbers.

At least he would have no difficulty in getting back, he reflected dully. Other things defined themselves. He saw where the small floorboards of the wagons had been ripped asunder by the outlaws in their search for hidden gold which they undoubtedly knew was being carried by each of the families. All of the people in the train apart from himself had either been killed or had gone to the extreme length of turning their guns on themselves, knowing what would lie in store for them if the outlaws took them alive.

Shuddering, he turned away from his examination of the wagons. In one of them he had located a cask of water and he filled his belly until he could hold no more, feeling the icy liquid shock a little of the life back into his bruised and battered body. Then he washed some of the dust and blood from his face and neck. The water swilled over him, stung his flesh as the mask of alkali cracked from his scorched skin. His temple ached intolerably under the touch of the water, but the bleeding had stopped and even washing away the encrusted blood did not start it again. Feeling a little better, able to see more clearly, he moved to the front of the wagon and succeeded in cutting one of the horses loose. Acting on impulse, he freed the others, realizing that they might starve to death if left tied to the smashed wagons. Swinging up into the improvised saddle, he clung to the reins with both hands, lying low over the horse's neck. The food and water he had packed into the saddlebag was all he could carry. Taking only one of the rifles and some cartridges, he left the grim scene of death and destruction, rode east out of the narrow valley. The cold night air revived him sufficiently as he rode into the flooding moonlight and twenty minutes later, he reached the bank of the river which they had crossed the previous day. The moonlight shone and glittered on the slow sweep of the water, breaking here and there into scattered shards of white light whenever ripples spread across the smooth surface.

He reined his mount, pondered whether to risk a night crossing in his condition, then decided against it. There was, he reckoned, no further danger to himself from the outlaws. They had got what they had come for and would have ridden out for their hiding place now, thinking everyone dead the in train.

Hobbling the horse as best he could in the loose earth, he stretched himself out on the ground, using the saddle for a pillow, resting on that side of his head which had not been hit. He found it difficult to sleep. The moon shone full into his face, and even when he closed his eyes against it, the brilliant white light still probed through the flesh of his eyelids. There was the distant wail of a coyote, rising and falling along a saw-edged scale. He heard it with a faint shiver of revulsion. It came again and was then answered from a different direction and from somewhere closer at hand. In spite of the tight control he held on his emotions, his hand reached out and his fingers curled tightly around the stock of the loaded rifle on the ground beside him.

Slowly, the moon wheeled across the cloudless night sky. Little shadows moved on the earth and in the near distance, there was the endless lapping of the water as it surged against the bank, eating at the soil, carrying it away in the current, depositing it somewhere many miles away, possibly in the distant Gulf of Mexico.

At length, his weary body found the sleep it craved. When he woke, his head still throbbing painfully, it was almost dawn. There was a pale metallic sheen to the east and the stars were dimming in that direction, although in the still dark-blue at the zenith and towards the mountains in the west, they still shone with a certain brightness and the moon was swinging low towards the skyline. He lay still for a long moment, not wanting to move, although knowing that he would have to. Then he stirred himself with an effort, rolled over on to his side and pushed himself up into a sitting position. He was still as weak as a wet kitten and the ache had spread down into his body now until there was scarcely a muscle or a limb that did not twitch as though his flesh was crawling.

He went down to the river's edge, knelt and drank deep of the water. It was muddy and tasted of sand, but it slaked his thirst and he felt a little better as he forced himself to stand. After eating a couple of slices of jerked beef cold, he went towards the horse, tightened the cinch under its belly, led it across to the water, then hauled himself weakly into the saddle. His vision blurred for a moment with the effort. Then he was able to see more clearly again. Digging in with the rowels of his spurs, he put the horse forward into the river. It edged forward slowly, uncertainly, seemed to hesitate for a moment, then stepped into the current as Tracey muttered a thin curse under his breath and raked metal across the animal's flanks. The current caught it almost at once and it went under for a moment, dragging him down with it, before it began to swim with the current. Savagely, cursing loudly, he hauled on the reins and slowly managed to turn it into the current, forcing it to track across the river to the opposite bank. Somehow, he made it, the horse clambering through the shallows there until it stood on dry land, water pooling from its belly.

Ahead of him lay the desert, mile after mile of white alkali. Soon, the sun would lift itself clear of the far horizon, a burning ball of fire in the still, clear heavens and there would be no shade for him from that rolling, eye-searing heat. Even in good physical condition a man could stand only so much of that terrible, ruthless pressure and in his weakened state it was doubtful if he could remain conscious through the long day which stretched ahead of him; yet he had to keep on moving, there was no place to stop and to have remained behind at the river would have only meant postponing the inevitable for a little longer, until his physical condition deteriorated even more and his chances of survival lessened.

He gigged the mount, hating himself for what he had to do to the horse, but knowing that now he had no choice in the matter. It was a case of keep moving or die. The horse started forward as it felt the sharp touch of the rowels on its flesh, ran on for a little while in the treacherous, drifting alkali, then slowed to a walking gait, head bowed a little. Pretty soon, the alkali would eat into its hooves, burning and blistering, working its way into tiny folds and cracks. He felt a little shiver go through him as he thought of what lay ahead, then gritted his teeth, hung on grimly to the reins and forced himself to sit upright in the saddle while everything swung and spun around him, the horizon tilting crazily from one side to another as blood rushed pounding sickenly to his head.

Minutes went by, long drawn-out nightmares, each made up of seconds of agony as the light around him brightened, and long shadows knifed into the narrow, shallow gullies in the desert. At last, the sun lifted clear of the horizon, flooding the desert with light, half-blinding him with its brilliance. He blinked his eyes several times, tried to force away the pounding ache in his head but found it impossible to do so.

He heard the soft shuffle of the horse through the

alkali, but there was no other sound apart from the drumming of blood in his ears. Screwing up his eyes, he let his body droop forward over the neck of the horse and lapsed into a state of semi-consciousness in which he scarcely knew anything that went on around him. All that he was conscious of was the fact that the horse continued to walk forward towards the glaring sun into that terrible expanse of whiteness.

By the time the sun had reached its zenith, throwing no shadows now on the desert, he was in a sorry way. The wound in his scalp had opened again and blood trickled down the side of his face. To add to his misery and discomfort, a host of tiny flies had appeared as if from nowhere, attracted by the smell of blood, swarming around him in their hundreds. biting at his flesh. But the pain from their bites somehow kept him from lapsing into unconsciousness, keeping him awake in the saddle. He stopped nowhere during those long hours of that first day. Hunger rumbled in his stomach and thirst dried up his mouth and throat, swelling his tongue until it seemed to be more than twice its normal size, moving rustily against his teeth. Occasionally, he sipped a few drops of water from his canteen, letting it swill around his mouth for a few moments before swallowing. But as time went on, his parched mouth simply soaked it up so that there was none left to go down his throat.

When evening came, and the sun was touching the tall hills far to the west of the Badlands, he felt the first faint stirrings of coolness on his scorched face and straightened up a little in the saddle. The air he drew into his aching lungs still felt as if it had been drawn across some vast furnace before it had reached him and his chest hurt with the agony of it. The snake-mottled twistings of the trail blurred in front of him, merging here and there into deeper shadow as the colours turned from vivid reds and oranges, into the steely blues of twilight. Now that the darkness was coming down, he began to cast about him for a place to camp, knowing that he could not continue through the night. The horse was almost at the end of its endurance now and there was no water to spare for it. He remembered the dried-up water courses he had seen on the journey westward across this desert and the first stirrings of defeat trembled in him.

Everywhere looked the same now. There was a soft haze lying over the desert, touching the low ridges where the wind had made eddies in the alkali. Then, off to the right, he saw a patch of green-brown, turned his mount towards it, peering into the growing dimness to ascertain what it was. It turned out to be a patch of tough wiry grass which somehow managed to suck a little moisture from the parched ground to survive. It was as good a place as any to make camp and he slid wearily from the saddle, holding on to the horse for a moment as his legs threatened to collapse under him. Drawing in a deep breath, he forced himself to remain upright, hobbled the horse as best he could, then lowered himself on to the grass. The sun dropped behind the mountain range with one last vivid explosion of scarlet and the night came swiftly out of the east.

Stretching himself out on the ground, he lay for what seemed an eternity, watching the sky darken over him, watching the first faint stars appear, then brighten slowly. The moon would come up later, he thought dully. He fingered the wound on his scalp. It still bled slowly and his fingers were wet with the stickiness of blood as he pulled them away, staring down at them in the darkness, trying to see the smears which he knew were on his fingertips. There was a deep and utter weariness in his body which transcended anything he had experienced before, even in the long and arduous campaigns against the Yankees.

How long he lay awake, he did not know. He saw the moon come up, sailing serenely into the clear heavens, and then he fell into an uneasy doze, merging on delirium, waking at intervals as pain throbbed through his skull. For a long while during the latter part of the night, he must have been only semi-conscious, and when dawn finally broke, he found he could hardly swallow, his throat on fire with thirst. The effort to get to his feet was almost too much for him. He had had no blanket and the temperature during the night had fallen almost to freezing point, leaving his bones stiff and sore.

The horse had not moved since he had hobbled him the previous evening. Some of the tough, springy grass had been cropped, but he reckoned there would have been little moisture or sustenance in that. Still, it was better than nothing, he reflected inwardly as he pulled himself up into the saddle with a wrench of his arm and shoulder muscles. The horse responded gamely as he touched spurs to it. Swaying stiffly from side to side in the saddle, body bruised and rubbed raw in places, he forced himself to sit tall and straight, probing the pale light of dawn with his glance, keeping the animal pointed in the right direction. Here, in this wilderness, it would be easy for a man to go around in circles until he and his mount were so weak they could go no further; and then there would be something for the buzzards which he could now make out in the heavens, sailing in wide circles on outspread wings. The shiver went through him again and it was only with a tremendous effort of will that he succeeded in forcing down the rising nausea in the pit of his stomach. He pulled a strip of dried beef from the saddle bag and chewed on it, trying to get a little comfort and moisture from it, working it around with his tongue. In the end, he was forced to spit it out, unable to swallow it. His throat muscles seemed corded and constricted, causing him pain whenever he attempted to swallow.

That day was worse than the other which had preceded it. If anything, the burning touch of the sun was more intense. Sweat streamed into his eyes and he felt as though his whole body was being slowly dehydrated, leaving him like a board that had been left out too long in the hot sun, twisted and warped, dried out, blackened inside, scorched outside. It was difficult to see now, with the sweat running down his wrinkled forehead into his eyes and the painful ache behind his temples growing steadily worse, until it was like a huge drum booming endlessly away inside his skull, vast throbbing echoes racing from one side of his head to the other, threatening to drown out every other sound.

The far edge of the wasteland seemed as distant as ever, receding from him no matter how long he travelled. Commonsense told him he ought not to keep on riding through the torrid heat of the high noon sun, but he kept going, driven on by something that went beyond sense, beyond reason. He rode more slowly now, making poor progress. Little eddies of the white, caustic dust lifted in the hot fingers of the wind, worked their way into the creases and folds of his skin, itching and irritating him. Mingling with the sweat that rolled down his face and back, it added to the discomfort of the terrible heat, caked his features behind a mask of grey from which only his eyes looked out, burning with fever.

It became impossible for him to sit upright in the saddle any longer. The air that he sucked into his lungs brought him no comfort, instead it seemed to be suffocating him. How much longer he would be able to go on like this, he did not know. Night seemed a long way off, and although the burning sun had passed its zenith now, was drifting westward in its long slide down the afternoon sky, the heat head increased rather than diminished. It pressed down on him from all sides, it was refracted in great dizzying waves from the glaring mirror of the alkali, it struck him forcibly no matter which way he tried to turn in the saddle.

That night, when he camped on the top of a low ridge that overlooked one of the dried-out water courses, he had to force himself to eat some of the beef and wash it down with what little water he had left in the canteen. This was the first time during this terrible nightmare of a ride that he realized he was so low on water. A man might go for a few days here without food and still survive but having no water was a very different matter. He shook his canteen, holding it close to his ear, trying to estimate how much water he had left, reckoned it could be no more than another half dozen mouthfuls. Then he would be without any and his life after that would be counted in hours, not days . . .

He woke while it was still dark, lay on his side, trying to recall where he was. He had been dreaming just before he woke, that he was back in the green hills and valleys of Missouri and the dream had been so vivid, had stuck in his mind, that for a long moment, he imagined he was still there and this strange, cold, flat world, made no sense to him. He forced himself to keep his eyes open, then pushed himself on to his hands and knees. Peering into the dimness, he stared down the gentle slope towards the old watercourse which he had seen the previous evening when he had made camp. Now, he could scarcely believe his eyes. There was water there, cool and crystal clear, flowing slowly in front of his astonished gaze. He could even pick out the sound of it, splashing over the small stones.

With a faint croaking gasp, he crawled forward towards it, fingers scrabbling in the dust. Less than three feet from him and he could almost touch it now. He reached out a trembling hand, thrust it forward and felt his fingers touch-dust, dry, cold dust that sifted in his hand. In spite of himself, he croaked a harsh curse, moved forward further, knew it for a mirage, an image conjured up by his fevered brain, having no existence in reality. Sobbing in his anger and frustration, he lay there for several moments on his stomach, trying to force rationality into his mind.

Somehow, he managed to get up into the saddle and continue on that long trek back east. He drifted in and out of delirium as the hours went under the slow gait of the horse and his body was incredibly weak from loss of blood and thirst. The punishment of the saddle became an endless, unbearable thing and at times, he felt his lips shaping wordless curses. A numbness held his legs and he felt a fear deep within him that perhaps the bullet wound on the side of his scalp had done far more damage to him than he had realized at first. Such a bone-shaking impact was bound to have had some effect, murmured a little voice at the front of his mind. He tried to forget that possibility as the day wore on. Vaguely through the shimmering heat haze, he tried to pick out the green land which he knew to exist somewhere on the edge of this alkali waste, but he could see nothing through the heat-shimmering glare that pervaded everything. He had the unshakeable feeling that he was simply wandering around in circles now, that the sun which had been earlier on his right was now to his left. He tried to give some attention to that thought, to hold on to it, but it kept drifting away and had no sense to it.

Sometime during the long afternoon, lifting his head with a jerk of his neck muscles, he thought he caught a glimpse of something moving in the far distance, a tiny string of black dots that moved slowly over the desert. He stared at them from beneath wrinkled brows, screwing up his eyes against the glare, but could not make out what they were, nor how far distant they happened to be and a little part of his mind, detached but oddly alert, told him that this was simply another mirage like the water he had seen that morning and he felt a grim and cold determination in him to ignore those dots, to tell himself that they did not really exist and there was no point in dwelling on them overmuch because madness lay that way.

Swaying unsteadily in the saddle, at times only just managing to hold on by clinging with all of his fading strength to the horse's neck, he tried to keep a hold on his buckling consciousness. It had taken them three days to cross the flats on that outward journey, he kept telling himself fiercely, and there was no reason why he ought not to be able to do the same. He didn't have to dig the wagons loose from the treacherous alkali as they had on that other journey, something which must have slowed their progress considerably. On the other hand, his mount was tired and weak. There had been no water for it since they had left the river and it was almost finished. Add that to the fact that he no longer knew if he was travelling in the right direction, and he knew with a growing certainty that he wasn't going to make it.

Aware again of the warm wetness oozing down the side of his head, he pulled the horse to a halt in one of the shallow depressions in the alkali. The sun was almost directly behind him now, beating down unhindered on the back of his neck, even though he had pulled the wide-brimmed hat down as far as possible in an attempt to give some shade on his neck.

He knew he could go no further now without a rest.

His legs and arms felt so weak he could scarcely move them and when he slid from the saddle, his knees buckled under him, no longer able to take his weight and he fell forward, feeling the scorching heat of the dust under his body, burning through his torn clothing. How long he lay there, he did not know, drifting in and out of unconsciousness. Once, he thought he heard voices somewhere off in the distance, dismissed the idea from his mind, rejecting it at once, knowing with some spark of consciousness that it was not possible for anyone to be there, that he was simply imagining it all in his mind.

A deep red mist floated across his vision and he wondered why the canteen slipped from nerveless fingers when he tried to lift it to his mouth. He knew that he was lying on the ground, flat on his back, staring up through slitted eyes at the glaring disc of the sun. Then something blotted it out, something that stood between him and the sun. He heard the harsh voice vaguely, as if it were speaking to him from a great distance, but he did not believe it when it said:

'Looks like some *hombre* who's been tryin' to make it back from the other side.'

He still felt disbelief in his voice, told himself this was not really happening at all. Even when the cold neck of a canteen was held to his lips and he felt his head being supported by a strong arm, with the cool water trickling down his throat he only half-believed that it was true.

He must have slipped into unconsciousness at that moment, for when he came round, an unguessable time later, the sun was still there, but his throat felt better and his tongue moved a little more freely between his teeth. He opened his eyes and focused them on the face that bent over him, looked beyond the face and saw the blue uniform which the man wore, grew aware that there were other men in the background, sitting or standing by their mounts.

With an effort, he sucked in a choking breath, tried to sit up. He heard the man saw sharply: 'He's coming round, Sergeant.'

A man got down from one of the horses and walked towards him, stood with legs braced well apart, said quietly, but firmly: 'Reckon you can ride now, mister? This is bad country and the sooner we're out of it, the better.'

He swallowed, nodded his head with an effort that sent pain stabbing into his brain, but the knowledge that he was not alone, that he had been found, was a powerful stimulant, enabled him to get to his feet, swaying drunkenly for a long moment it was true, but to stand unaided, shrugging off the helping hand which had gripped his elbow tightly.

'I can make it all right,' he said hoarsely, his voice little more than a harsh croak, forced up from the depths of his throat.

'Your mount is just about tuckered, but I reckon he'll carry you as far as you have to go.'

Tracey felt a new strength in his limbs as he climbed up into his saddle, gave a quick nod to the others, then fell in with them. His eyes still hurt as though they were on fire, and the dust had worked its way under the lids, stinging each time he blinked. But the long drink of cold water had eased the fire in his stomach and he found himself able to think a little more clearly. He did not question the miracle which had led this troop of soldiers to him in the middle of that vast expanse of alkali. Carefully, he rolled his head to the right, saw that the sun was dropping away now, horizonward, on the far side of the flats.

They made no stops and when dusk came, they were almost on the edge of the alkali and in the growing dimness, pushing his gaze ahead, Tracey was able to make out the rolling hills and ridges, covered first with the tough, springy grass and then with mesquite and scrub oak, before lifting into more lush green hills half a mile or so away.

They made camp in a grassy clearing at the side of the trail, hobbling their mounts and building a fire. Tracey sat on the edge of the clearing, smoking a cigarette he had rolled from the tobacco one of the men had given him. The crackling brilliance of the roaring fire lifted high as more wood and dead-fall twigs were tossed on to it and there was the sizzling of meat in a pan, filling the air with an appetising aroma, heightening the gnawing ache in the bottom of his stomach. The cigarette held its satisfaction to the very end and he looked about him, at the dancing red light reflected against the sombre darkness of the surrounding trees.

The tall man with the broad Sergeant's stripes on his tunic came forward, squatted down beside him, legs thrust out to the blazing fire. 'Care to talk about it?' he said softly, his face bearing a serious expression.

'Not much to tell,' Tracey said. 'The name's Tracey Dillman. I was with the last wagon train to go across the Flats four or five days back. We got to the river and then headed for the valley between the bluffs, figuring we'd make good progress once we were through. We'd heard of the outlaw bands operatin' in these parts, but when the other scout and myself found a train that had obviously been ambushed only a few weeks previously, we reckoned the chances were good that the gang that had done it, were fifty or sixty miles away. Instead, they were lyin' in wait for us halfway through the pass, hit us with rifle fire without warnin'.'

The other let his glance wander to the rifle by Tracey's side. 'I see you had some Spencers with you.'

Tracey gave a quick, brief nod. 'We figured they might help to turn the trick if we did run into trouble. But we never reckoned there would be so many of 'em. Must've been thirty or forty men in that bunch that hit us.'

'That wouldn't be far from the mark, I guess,' acknowledged the other. 'We hear of these gangs, but we ain't managed to catch up with any of 'em yet. They have men watchin' all the trails in these parts, maybe as far back as New Orleans. They'd know every move you made since you pulled out.'

'I figured that to be so,' nodded Tracey. He flicked the butt of the smoke into the fire, leaned his back against the tree behind him. 'I reckon I was lucky. A shot creased my skull and knocked me cold. When I came round, there was nobody left alive with the train and the outlaws had gone. I took one of the horses from the wagons and tried to work my way back. It was further than I'd figured.'

'That's bad country out yonder,' affirmed the other. He leaned forward, speared a piece of bacon with the point of his knife, slid it on to one of the plates and handed in to Tracey. 'Help yourself to the beans,' he said, inclining his head in the direction of the pan over the fire.

Tracey filled his plate, ate slowly, knowing the penalty that had to be paid if one ate too quickly on a stomach that had been empty as long as his. The food tasted delicious, better than anything he had eaten before. He did not look up until the plate was clean and the mug of coffee drunk.

The Sergeant waited until he had finished, then said quietly: 'We're just finishing our patrol. On our way back to camp. Reckon it'd be better if you was to come along with us, get the doctor there to take a look at that head of yours. No sense in tryin' to keep on ridin' with a wound like that which needs attention. Besides, you ain't got anythin' important to go back for, I guess.'

'Guess you're right,' Tracey felt tired, but this time, it was a natural weariness and not the feeling of delirium and semi-consciousness that had plagued him for the past two nights.

He took the blanket that one of the men held out to him, spread it out a little distance from the fire and rolled himself in it, looking up at the stars where they glittered through gaps in the leaves overhead. The earth was soft and there was a moist smell in his nostrils, not the harsh, acrid, burnt-out scent of the Alkali Flats. He fell asleep at once, head pillowed in his arm and slept soundly without waking once, until he was roused at dawn the next day by one of the soldiers shaking him gently by the shoulder.

'Time to be movin', mister,' he said, not unkindly. 'Just time for a bite to eat and then we move out. I figured you needed plenty of rest so I let you sleep on.'

'Thanks.' Tracey sat up, looking about him. The camp was already breaking up, and he had slept through it all. His head felt better and the ache in his body was no longer as bad as it had been the previous day. He ate the breakfast which was handed to him, washing it down with the hot, strong coffee.

Fifteen minutes later, they rode out of the clearing, heading north into densely wooded country, along a broad trail that twisted in and out of the trees, with the deep green gloom all about them where no sunlight ever managed to filter down through the trees and the smell of pines was thick and sweet in their nostrils, pine needles underfoot muffling the sound of their mounts. The trees around them were mostly of first-growth pine, slender trunks stretching up straight for perhaps twenty or thirty feet without blemish, then forming a wide umbrella of leaves and branches.

Near eleven or twelve o'clock, they moved out of the timber, down the trail that led over a low rise, into a valley below, green and lush. Here, even the sunlight seemed to have lost that harsh, glaring quality which it had possessed out there in the Flats. It was still warm, but the earth seemed to soak up the heat, taking most of it out of the air, leaving a softer warmth and radiance.

'Where does this trail go?' he asked, turning his head and glancing at the Sergeant who rode beside him.

'On to the outpost,' said the other, pointing a hand into the blue-hazed distance. 'From there, it continues north until it meets up with one of the stage trails going back east to New Orleans. You can take that road once you're fit enough to travel.'

'Fair enough,' agreed Tracey. He fell silent, letting his gaze roam over the stretching greenness, pausing at times to remember what had happened back there in that narrow valley between the tall sandstone bluffs which had trapped them as surely as the outlaws. The rising anger in his body was not easily thrust away. There was a strange restlessness in him, urging him to go back and destroy those men who had perpetrated this act of treachery and violence, but he knew that to be impossible at the moment. Maybe in New Orleans, he might be able to get in with another wagon train heading west and next time, he would be ready for any eventuality.

Major Allenton sat tall and erect behind the desk, his military bearing visible in every line of him, from the iron-grey hair and trim moustache, to the cut of his uniform.

'Sit down, Mr Dillman,' he said, his tone stiff and precise, the words clipped in the manner of a man used to giving commands, and having them obeyed. 'I understand from Sergeant Heenan that you were found wandering around in the Flats, delirious. Perhaps you'd like to tell me everything that happened.'

'But I've already explained all that to your Sergeant on the way here,' said Tracey harshly. He lowered himself into the chair and sat straight in it, facing the other across the desk.

For a moment, the grey brows lifted slightly, the other permitted himself a wintry smile, but there was no mirth in it and it never reached his eyes. He said softly, but with steel showing through: 'I realize that, but I want you to tell everything to me, missing out nothing.' He held up his right hand as Tracey made to begin, silencing him for a moment.

'Perhaps before you start, I ought to explain my position in this matter. We are a company at this fortified outpost detailed not only to defend the borders against Indians, but also against outlaws. We know there are bands roaming the territory to the west of here and that they sometimes operate this side of the Flats, but so far we've been unable to trail any of them to their hideouts and until we can do that and in strength, we don't have a chance in hell of stopping them. We need all of the information we can get about them and as you appear to be the only survivor of this attack, your testimony can be of extreme value to us. Hence, I want you to repeat to me everything you told Sergeant Heenan, missing nothing, you understand.'

'Very well.' Sitting forward a little in his chair, Tracey went over all that had happened from the moment the wagon train had crossed the wide river on the western side of the alkali desert, until the time when he had come to, finding himself the only person left alive out of the entire train.

The Major listened to him intently, not interrupting him once, then he sat back in his chair, staring straight in front of him, fingertips placed together in the shape of a tent. For a moment, it was as if he were not aware of Tracey's presence there in the quiet room, then he said softly, stirring himself a little:

'What you've told me bears out much of what we knew before. They have their hideout somewhere to the north and west of the point where you were ambushed. It's rough country there, full of swamp and bayou and there are a thousand places where they could hide and we'd never be able to smoke 'em out.' He got slowly to his feet, pacing back and forth behind the desk, his hands clasped tightly behind his back.

'If only we knew where they were,' he said thinly, speaking as if to himself. 'But like the wagon trains, they know our every move too.'

'You think they may have a man inside the outpost, Major?' asked Tracey, in surprise.

'It's a thought which I've considered on one or two occasions,' admitted the other, 'and it wouldn't be the first time it's happened in one of our outposts. There are settlers and trappers here all the year round, drifting in and out whenever the mood takes them. We don't stop them. That's one of the reasons we're here, to afford them protection. But it does mean that we could have an enemy in our midst and not know it. Even if we suspected anyone, it would be a difficult thing to prove it.'

Sitting himself down in his chair again, the other took a cigar from a humidor on his desk, offered one to Tracey, smiled a little once again as the other shook his head. He paused to light the cigar, blew smoke into the air over his head, and continued: 'We've heard the name Laredo and also Carrico. They seem to be leaders of this band of outlaws. Whether they really exist or not is another matter, but I'd be prepared to stick my neck out and say that they do.' The other scowled hard at Tracey. 'You didn't happen to see any of these men who attacked the train?'

'Only those who were left lying there after the attack,' said the other softly. 'We killed several of 'em before they finished the job.'

'I guessed that. But it's not likely that either of these men, if it was their band, would put themselves in too much danger. They'd leave all of the dirty work to their men. They take the spoils and divide it to suit themselves.'

'They'd have plenty from that train,' Tracey told him tightly. 'I reckon there must've been close on two hundred thousand dollars in gold among those wagons and they seemed to have stripped the lot.'

The Major snorted. He clasped his fingers tightly together, interlacing them. The cigar stuck out at an angle from his tightly-pressed lips. For a moment, the other eyed him tautly. Then he removed the cigar from his lips and tapped the ash into a tray in front of him. 'I don't aim to send any of my men out there hunting down this bunch, unless I know a little more about their hideout,' he went on. 'There are too many of them to tangle with without preparations.'

'Wouldn't it be easier to send an escort with the wagon trains until they're well through this territory?'

'We've thought of that too and been forced to dismiss the idea,' said the other stonily. 'If we tried that, they've got men to warn them of it, and there would be no sign of them along the trail. Besides, once we started that every wagon master moving a train out of this territory would demand an escort and I don't have the men to do that. We're not here to wet-nurse these wagon trains across country all the way to California, we're only here to keep law and order on the frontier to the best of our ability. And at the moment, the Government obviously doesn't see its way clear to send me enough men even for that task.'

Tracey watched the other closely, watched the flurry of strange, unguessable things come to his eyes and harden the set of his features.

'Is there any way I can help?'

The other shot him a cold, clear glance. 'Any reason why you should want to take part in this fight?' he asked keenly. 'This is something we have to take care of by any means we have at our disposal. Don't reckon there's any reason for a civilian to take part in it.'

'I'm in it whether I like it or not,' Tracey retorted tightly. 'Those critters killed everybody on that wagon train but me. I'd have been killed too if my luck hadn't held out to the end. I want a chance to get even with those polecats, and I figure I've got it comin'. The man who led that wagon train gave me a chance when I needed it most. He was a Yankee, but he didn't sneer at the colour of my uniform as so many men did. He was a good and honest man who believed in a dream. and that he could take those people through to California. They didn't make it, and I aim to see that the killers who stopped 'em pay for what they did.'

'Well now,' began the other slowly, chewing around the edge of his cigar. 'I seem to have misjudged you a little, Mr Dillman. I had you figured for a saddle tramp, hitching your gun to any man who paid a high enough price for it. Seems I was wrong.' He sat back in his chair, regarding Tracey contemplatively.

Outside, there was the sound of men drilling in the large courtyard inside the thick wooden stockade. The heavy sound of booted heels on the hard earth was a rhythmic, muffled tread of men marching in step. Now and again, there came the sharp bark of a command, a change in the step.

A moment later, the Major got to his feet, stood looking down at Tracey for a long moment, then said softly, 'I reckon you'd better get that head wound seen to first. We can talk about this more fully when you feel better. In the meantime, you're welcome to stay at the post for as long as you wish.'

'Thank you, Major.' For a moment, Tracey felt a little surprise at the way in which the other had accepted his point of view so readily. He had expected the other to argue about it, instead he had aquiesced without hesitation.

Outside, an orderly took him over to the small hospital on the outpost. It was merely a long room with iron beds set down each side and a harrassed looking man who turned out to be the doctor. The orderly spoke to him in a low undertone for a moment, motioning in Tracey's direction, then saluted stiffly and left. The doctor came over to him.

'Sit down here,' he said wearily, 'and I'll take a look at that wound of yours. Bullet wound, eh?'

'That's right,' Tracey nodded, said nothing further, not wishing to go into the story again after having told it twice.

Holding his head a little to one side, he sat bolt upright in the chair while the other examined the wound. After washing it, he said. 'Seems to be healing up nicely. No sign of infection there which is the main thing. Lucky for you that you have a thick skull there or you'd have been dead by now. That bullet must've glanced off the bone without shattering it. Hold still, while I put a bandage on. Then you'll have to rest up for a week or so, get your strength back. You've lost a good deal of blood.' He paused, wound the bandage tightly around Tracey's forehead. 'You weren't figuring on goin' any place in a hurry, were you?' he asked.

With an effort, Tracey shook his head. 'I'll ride on back to New Orleans soon as I'm able,' he answered, 'but there's no hurry about it.'

Tight-lipped, the doctor nodded. 'You'll find life out here quiet, but that's the kind you'll need for this to heal right.'

In the days that followed, each one running into the other, the wound along the side of his skull healed and the strength returned to his body. But although there was little outward sign now of what he had experienced, there was a deep scar within him which had not healed, which would not heal until he had met those men who had attacked that train, and had evened the score with them. This was the thought that burned in his mind as he stood in the shadow of the high wooden walls and watched the soldiers drilling in the courtyard. In particular, he was interested in the rifles they used. More modern than the Spencer rifles he had carried on that ill-fated ride to the west, they looked to be a far better model than anything he had seen before.

He had a word with the Corporal in charge of the small armoury there. The other nodded, handed him one of the weapons.

'This is the Henry,' said the other warmly, evidently glad to find someone as interested in weapons as he himself. 'It's a development of the Spencer which the cavalrymen used during the war. They still use 'em around, but we're gettin' these more and more now. Handier when it comes to rapid firing, but it still ain't the best. Now if they could only make the whole thing automatic, from firing one cartridge, ejecting it and making the next one ready for firin'. That would be a real man's weapon.'

'You reckon they ever will have one like that?' asked Tracey, deeply interested. Already, his quick and fertile mind was looking ahead, foreseeing the possibilities of a rifle with those qualifications. A gun that would fire off several bullets in rapid succession, with only the one movement to reload. That would be something.

'There is talk that they've got a new gun, but I ain't seen any of 'em,' said the other. 'Reckon though it'd take a lot to improve on these.' The other hefted the Henry rifle in his hands with an almost loving care. 'We need a quick firing rifle if we're to tame this goddamned country. Too many Indians and outlaws still on the loose and a good rifle will be the only advantage we'd have if we came on 'em in force.'

'You think the Army will get these new guns first, when they're developed?'

The Corporal pursed his lips in thought. 'Hard to say. They may decide that any legitimate frontiersman will need one. Guess it's the right of every man to protect himself.'

'I reckon so.' Tracey stared down at the Henry repeating rifle glistening dully in the sunlight. A good weapon, he reflected, but he felt sure there would soon be another that would be far better in many respects, Once he had a gun such as he imagined, he felt sure there would be no need for him to fear anyone.

He thought about that all the time he stayed at the outpost. The wound in his head was soon better, the bandages removed, the hair growing again over the place where the bullet had sliced off his scalp. There came a day when he knew he could stay there no longer. Saddling up his mount, he rope out of the stockade, through the wide gates, out on to the widening trail which led east in the direction of New Orleans.

FOUR

False Accusation

Word about the ambushing of the wagon train had passed on ahead into New Orleans and when he rode into the town, Tracey guessed there might be some folk there who would want to know what happened, who would wish to question the lone survivor of that train so that the same thing might not happen to anyone else driving out west; but even so, he was not prepared for the coldness, the veiled yet easily discernible hostility which his presence evoked at the hotel where he put up, even in the street and especially at the bar when he went into one of the saloons. It had never occurred to him that some of the blame for what had happened might become attached to him, yet he knew this to be the case now. It was the wariness brought on by this hostility, that made him bitter, rubbed raw, as he left his hotel room and walked down into the street in the late afternoon sun. There was a small wagon train in the street close to the levee where the other one had been all that time ago.

How long ago was it in reality? he wondered dully. It seemed like years and yet it could only have been a couple of months, three at the most, since they had set out, with Gideon Carter in the lead, sitting on the tongue of his wagon as if he owned the whole of the country, confident that they would get through, not knowing then that only one out of the three or four dozen on the train would get back alive.

The deep weariness was back in him, and he felt that odd, though familiar, tremor in his limbs as he made his way slowly along the street, acutely aware of the dark glances he got now and then, the way in which some of the people who evidently recognized him, deliberately stepped out of his path so that he might not come into contact with them. This was something he would have to fight, and soon; yet he did not know how to begin.

Turning in through the batwing doors of one of the saloons, leaving the heat of the afternoon behind and stepping into the cool dimness of the bar-room, he felt every nerve tensed and alerted, every muscle coiling a little as one of the men at the bar, a big, hulking fellow, open necked shirt revealing the dark, corded tan of an outdoor life, clearly a farmer of some kind, possibly with the wagon train – turned and said in a loud voice:

'Bartender. I didn't know you served trash like this here.'

'Now steady on, Matt,' said the man behind the bar, his voice a little unsteady. He let his glance flicker in Tracey's direction, 'I don't want any trouble in here, you understand.'

'There won't be any trouble, so long as he keeps remarks like that to himself,' said Tracey harshly. He moved over to the bar, ignoring the big man, stood with his elbows hooked on to the polished top, nodded to the bartender as the other came sidling over to him.

'What'll it be?' asked the other, his features twisted a little into a vaguely frightened grimace.

'Whiskey,' Tracey said. He stood there with his side to the farmer, apparently oblivious of his presence, but watching the man closely out of the corner of his eye, seeing the other's reflection in the large glass mirror at the back of the bar. The other had not taken his eyes off him, his face twisted into a vicious, snarling scowl. There was no doubt the other was spoiling for a fight. It was clearly visible in every line of his body, in the tightly-balled fists hanging loosely by his sides, in the set of his jaw, thrust forward aggressively, in the narrowed eyes, the shoulders hunched forward.

The bartender placed the whiskey bottle and a glass in front of Tracey, then moved away hurriedly, his face scared, dabbing with his cloth at the counter as he left.

'You heard what I said, bartender. We come here to drink with decent folk, not with traitorous sidewinders who sell out a wagon train to outlaws.'

Tracey tightened his lips, teeth biting deep. He threw back the whiskey, felt the raw liquor burn the back of his throat on its way down. Slowly, he turned to face the other.

'You're hankerin' for trouble, friend,' he said slowly, forming his words clearly and distinctly. He had seen the other's bearing and attitude many times in the past, knew what they portended. The man was battle-scarred and capable-looking, a man who had met violence and survived it and Tracey felt certain that most of the violence had been on the other's own making. He looked the type who preferred to settle an argument with his fists rather than with a gun.

'You're durned right I'm lookin' for trouble,' snarled the other viciously. 'I'm particular who I drink with and you ain't the kind I like to have around when I'm drinking.'

Insolently and cool, Tracey said: 'Then I reckon you can always go someplace else for your whiskey.'

The other muttered a strong oath, moved a couple of paces away from the bar. His glance dropped to the twin guns at Tracey's waist, but there was no fear or apprehension in his look.

'I wondered if you'd ever have the gall to come ridin' back here after what you did,' he said tightly. 'And I promised all of the others that if you did, I'd be the first to rub your nose in the dirt. Then they could do what they liked with you. Reckon the best thing would be to string you up from the nearest tree.'

'Reckon you'd better back off,' Tracey warned. His hands were a few inches above the guns at his waist. 'I don't want to have to kill you. I don't even know you, but if you try to push me, I'll do what I have to.'

The man paused, grinning thinly. He half turned his head to the rest of the men standing near the bar. He said loudly so that everybody in the room could hear: 'Listen to him. He's responsible for the deaths of those men and women and children on that last train and now he wants to use his guns on an unarmed man. I figured that would be the way he fights.'

There was to be no alternative for Tracey. He knew what would come even before it happened. The other was committed to fight and no matter what his feelings were in the matter, Tracey knew he could not use his guns on the other man, even though there might be a small Derringer hidden under one armpit, ready for use once he shucked his own gunbelt.

The farmer started forward, moving lightly on the balls of his feet in spite of his size and weight. A born fighter, he had clearly been through many battles like this, would be a rough and dirty fighter.

'Better shuck that belt unless you want to shoot me down in cold blood,' growled the other, coming on without pause. 'Because I aim to smash you with my bare hands.'

There was nothing else Tracey could do in the circumstances. Slowly, he unclasped the heavy belt, let it drop loosely on to the floor to one side of his legs, and squared up to the other. He had been in several rough-house brawls himself and could handle his fists as well as the next man. Consequently, he knew what was coming from the other a split second before the man did anything.

The farmer moved forward slowly, one foot placed carefully in front of the other, talking all the time he moved, sometimes addressing his remarks to Tracey and at other times to the men lounging along the bar, watching the coming fight with a frank and open interest.

It was an old trick, a stratagem to keep Tracey's attention fixed, to lull him into a sense of false security, until the other feinted with his right fist and struck hard with his left, possibly hitting low in an attempt to get in an early crippling blow. Tracey waited for him, watching the man's eyes narrowly, knowing that he was the kind who would telegraph his punches, giving that split second of warning before he threw a blow. Rocking slightly on his toes, he watched as the other moved to one side, bent low, swinging up all the way from his knees. It was easy to sidestep that blow, to move out of range of the tightfisted knuckles and hammer in a solid jolt to the other's face as he swayed off balance.

He felt the other's nose split under the solid impact and blood spurted down the farmer's square face. He had been hurt, but not too badly. Shaking his head to clear it, he paused in his tracks for a moment, sucked air down into his barrel chest, then came on again, swinging wildly this time, throwing blows from every direction. One caught Tracey on the side of the face, grazing along the line of the recently healed bullet wound. For a second, a little tremor of apprehension ran through him. Had that hard-knuckled blow re-opened that wound where the newly formed flesh was still tender?

With that thought uppermost in his mind, momentarily troubling him, he failed to see the blow that arced on him from the other's left fist. It struck him full on the chest, almost caved in his ribs under the shattering impact. All of the air seemed to have been knocked from his lungs. He heard it wheeze out through his open lips, felt the stab of pain, then gave ground hurriedly, covering up with his arms and elbows, taking the following flurry of blows on them, suffering little punishment, forcing the other to expend his energy in doing little damage. Gradually, the feeling came back into his bruised chest. He drew in a breath without it hurting quite so much and his vision had cleared.

He could hear the quick, rasping grunts of the other

man, guessed that in spite of his outward build, the man was out of condition a little. Already, the pace seemed to be beginning to tell on him. He grinned viciously to himself, swung a savage blow at the other's face, felt his knuckles graze on the point of the farmer's chin, snapping his head back on his shoulders. The man grunted, and it was now his turn to back away under the furious onslaught of blows that Tracey rained on him. The man was rocked. He tried to twist himself out of the way, but the hard punches sank into his belly and his face turned a pasty grey under the brown tan. His eyes began to roll a little showing the whites as he gave a tiny bleat of pain, fell back until his shoulders were jammed hard against the edge of the bar. For the first time, the look of impending defeat came over his hard granite features. He sucked in his lips, tried to shake a little of the blood from his squashed nose as it trickled down into his mouth.

Then Tracey made a mistake. He moved too close to one of the other men standing by the bar. Without warning, the man put out a foot, twisted his spurs so that they caught in the other's ankle, pitching him backward. With a savage, bull-like roar, the farmer came in, arms flailing, colliding heavily with Tracey, using his superior weight to bear the other back. Tracey went down, unable to maintain his balance as his foot was hooked away from under him. He hit the ground hard with the other on top of him, fingers gouging for his eyes, nails raking over his cheeks.

His breath was pantingly close to Tracey's face and he tried to turn his head away, but it was impossible for him to do so. Instinct made him lower his head on to his chest, making it difficult for the man to get at his eyes, but he knew that he would have to throw the other off soon, or he would be finished. The man meant to break him with his bare hands and nothing else would satisfy him. He meant it to be a slow and agonizing end.

Feeling his arms free, Tracey locked them tightly around the man's middle, tightening his hands together in the small of the man's back, squeezing with all of his strength, forcing the farmer to one side. His head drummed and throbbed painfully but he heard the other gasp as the breath was crushed from his lungs by the bear hold around him. Writhing, the other tried to pull himself free of the encircling grip, but was unable to do so. Now the tables had been turned. There was nothing the heavier man could do to wriggle free. He drew back his lips in a snarling grin of pain, eyes squeezed shut in his head, brow furrowed with agony and effort. The sweat stood out on his forehead, began to trickle down into his eyes and along the side of the beak nose.

Pain and suffocation made the other grunt as he fought to drag air down into his aching lungs. Tracey felt the man's hold on him slacken as the pain grew more intense in the big farmer's body. The man was fighting with everything he had now. Tracey felt the other's leg go back, guessed what was coming a split second before the man tried to knee him in the bottom of the stomach. He twisted savagely to one side, rolling the other on to his side, then flopping on top of him.

Madly, the other struggled, but to no avail. His eyes bulged wide in his head, his mouth was open slackly now, lips twisted, uneven teeth showing, tobacco stained and broken. Tracey let him lie like that for a while, until he got his own breath back, then he suddenly released his hold, stepped back, swinging up to his feet. For long seconds, the man lay on the floor of the saloon in front of him, sucking air greedily into his heaving chest. Then he seemed to realize the full vulnerability of his position, for he curled up, rolled away and got slowly and heavily to his feet, swaying now, one eye half shut, but his fists were still doubled up, swinging leadenly at his sides as he came lumbering forward. There was scarcely any strength in the first blow he swung at Tracey, but it was evident that he was trying to edge the other over to the bar where one of the other cronies of his could get in another blow and turn the trick for him again. But Tracey was not going to fall for that routine again. He had been bitten that way once in this fight and he would not be caught on the wrong foot again. He guessed that everyone in the saloon was against him, had even made out the shouts and yells of encouragement which had come from the men ranged against the bar during the first few minutes of the fight when he seemed to be getting the worst of it. Now that the farmer seemed to be losing, the yells were becoming more and more derisive, but they were still designed to force the other to keep coming forward, and there were no shouts of encouragement for him.

He stepped back a little, saw the look of triumph that crossed the farmer's face, then swung nimbly to one side, backed into the middle of the room, circling his adversary. Baulked in his intentions, the other suddenly threw all caution to the winds, determined to finish the fight with one haymaker that would have killed Tracey had it landed on its target. As it was, he felt the wind of the bunched fist sliding past his head, then he side-stepped neatly and threw three hard punches at the other, the first two in the soft of the belly, and the last on the tip of the man's jaw. The farmer uttered a little grunt as he ducked into the last punch, sagged at the knees, all of the starch gone from his legs by that blow. For good measure, as he fell forward against his knees, Tracey hit hard with the edge of his hand on the man's neck. A weaker neck would have been broken by the shuddering force of that blow. As it was, the man fell forward limply, knocked cold by the rabbit punch. He hit the floor with a dull thump and lay still, one hand outstretched over Tracey's gunbelt. Bending swiftly, still aware of the thumping pain in his temples, he picked up the belt and fastened it around his middle, turning slowly to face the rest of the men ranged along the bar.

He had expected some further trouble from them, had not thought they would have even given him the chance to buckle on his gunbelt. Then he saw that they were staring down at the man lying on the floor, his legs half under one of the tables. Lifting his glance, Tracey looked beyond them, saw the shotgun held firmly in the bartender's hands, covering all of the men there. When he saw that Tracey had his own guns on, he lowered the gun.

Thinly, he said: 'If you did what they say you did, I wish he'd killed you. But I'm always ready to give a man the benefit of the doubt and I like an even fight. These critters would've pulled a gun on you when you knocked him out. Better fight your battle with 'em now if they want to step up against you.'

Tracey gave the other a brief nod of thanks. It was more than he had expected from anyone. It showed that not everyone in New Orleans was prepared to accept what they heard as hear-say and condemn him without a word in his own defence. His ice-cold glance swept along the ranks of the men in front of him. There was a mute question in that look and a strangely cynical grin spread over his lips as he saw the way they turned their glances away from him, not able to meet his look. There would be little trouble from them now, he reflected. He wiped the back of his hand over his mouth, stepped back to the bar and picked up the whiskey bottle by the neck, poured a stiff shot into his glass and drank it down fast. It brought a warm glow into his stomach and he felt better. If this was going to be the sort of welcome he got no matter where he went in this town, maybe it was not going to be worth his while staying on, he decided. After all, New Orleans was not the only town where the wagon trains came in, ready for the long drive across country to California. He ought to be able to pick up one further to the north, perhaps at Natchez.

He poured a second drink, sipped it more slowly this time, then turned to some of the men at the bar. 'Reckon you'd better bring him round and then get him out of here,' he said in a silky tone. 'If I see him around again, I might not be so condescending as to shuck my gunbelt just for his benefit. Better warn him the next time he wants to make any remarks like that, he'd best be ready to use a gun, because I will.'

Two of the men moved away from the bar, caught the farmer by the heels and hauled him out through the batwing doors and down the sidewalk. The doors swung shut behind them.

Tracey turned and motioned to the bartender. The other came over slowly, a little uncertain of himself, not sure whether he had acted rightly or wrongly when he had stopped those men from shooting him down without warning.

'This story that's being spread around town about me sellin' out those settlers,' he said sharply. 'Any idea who started it?'

The man shook his head. There was a look of something akin to fear at the back of his eyes. 'Seems that everybody knows about it,' he said in a faintly quavering tone. 'Don't know who might've started it though. We did hear there'd been one survivor and that he was holeing up at one of the military outposts, but nobody knew who he was until Indian Pete came into town, about a week ago. He said it was you, out there at the outpost and he reckoned you'd be ridin' back into New Orleans pretty soon.'

'This Indian Pete,' Tracey said. 'You know where I can find him?'

'If he's still here, reckon he'll be in that shack at the back of the livery stables down the street a couple of hundred yards.'

'Thanks.' Tracey tossed a coin on to the counter, turned towards the door, then paused and glanced back. 'This *hombre* often come into town like this?'

'Indian Pete?' The other raised thick, bushy brows. 'Sure, see him every four, five weeks, maybe. Why d'you ask?'

'Nothin' important. Just a hunch I've got,' said Tracey. He turned and walked out into the street.

The whiskey had brought a feeling of well-being into his mind and body, and not even the battering he had received a while earlier, could take that feeling away as he walked slowly in the direction of the stables. The roadway dust lifted around him as he walked, sharp in his nostrils. He passed a public watering trough and debated whether to pause and wash the dirt and grime from his face and neck, then decided against it. He wanted a talk with this man who seemed to know so much about him; a man who came into New Orleans pretty regularly if the bartender had told the truth; a man who could learn a lot by keeping his eyes and ears open whenever the wagon trains were preparing to move out and who could get that important information back to the outlaws in the hills to the west.

He found the tumble-down shack at the rear of the livery stable just as the bartender had mentioned. The roof slanted so low that it almost touched the ground in places and the door hung on rusted hinges, creaking a little as he touched it with his hand and pushed it open, stepping inside with a wary alertness. He knew by some sixth sense, that there was someone in the gloom, even before he could make out the figure lying on the blanket against the far wall.

The other came instantly to his feet with a startled oath, reached out a hand for the rifle that lay on the floor beside him, then froze at once as Tracey said: 'Do that and you're a dead man.'

A pause, then the other said in a low, hushed tone. 'What do you want with me, stranger?'

'You Indian Pete?' he asked tersely, levelling the gun on the other as the man still cast a quick look towards his rifle.

'That's right.' Black eyes watched him warily as he advanced further into the room.

'You know me?' Tracey asked, not once removing his glance from the other.

The man scrutinised him for a long moment, then shook his head. 'No.'

'The name is Dillman, Tracey Dillman.' He saw the instant recognition in the other's hard stare at the mention of his name. 'I'm the man you've been spreadin' these tales about around town. Seems to me that you and me had better have a little talk.'

He thrust the Colt back into its holster, but was still ready

to pounce as the other bent swiftly, fingers curled to grab
for the rifle. Tracey's foot lashed out, the toe of his boot
catching the other sharply on the wrist. The rifle was
hurled, clattering, into the far corner of the hovel and the
other straightened up with a muttered curse, not touching
his injured wrist but with a look of feral hatred in the black
eyes.

'That's better,' said Tracey in a glacial tone. 'You
must've been at the outpost while I was there to have
heard about me at all.'

'I was at the outpost,' affirmed the other thinly. He
lowered himself to the blanket and sat cross-legged, hands
folded in front of him.

Tracey tried to guess at the other's age, but it was impossible. He looked to be sixty or seventy at least, his face wrinkled with many lines, eyes glittering brightly in his head.

'And before that – where were you then?'

'I was in the forests near the outpost,' said the other
woodenly. 'I hunt and trap, sell my furs here in New
Orleans.'

'And between times, maybe you pass along information
to Carrico and Laredo, warn them when a wagon train is
getting ready to move out, tip them off as to how many
men will be travellin' with it, how many rifles they'll have
and which trail they'll be takin'.'

'That is not true. I do not know either of these men of
whom you speak,' said the other dully. 'I am a trapper,
nothing more. I know nothing of wagon trains or rifles.'

'That is exactly what I thought you would say.' Tracey
nodded, showing no surprise at the other's words. It was
not likely that the other would admit to working in
cahoots with the outlaws; and yet there seemed no way of
proving any of this, certainly he doubted if anything he
could do, any threat he could utter, would make the other
talk. Merely threatening him with a gun would not be a
sufficient inducement to loosen his tongue. These Indians
had no fear of death and a man of his years even less so.

'Maybe if I was to take you to the outpost, get the Major

to use his ways of makin' people talk, he could get some-thin' out of you.'

The other said nothing, simply continued to stare in front of him, eyes unblinking. Tracey reached a sudden decision. He had little reason to stay here in New Orleans with the feelings as high against him as they were at the moment, but back at the outpost, this man might be made to tell what he knew and there was the possibility that if the Major could be persuaded to keep him prisoner at the outpost for a little while, they could get a wagon train through without Carrico or his killers knowing that it was on the way.

Bending, he pulled the man to his feet. 'You're comin' back to the outpost with me,' he said tightly. 'Even if you don't talk, we can at least keep you where you can do no more harm.'

'No,' said the other harshly. 'I will not go with you. I must remain here and—' Scarcely had he finished speak-ing, than he twisted like an eel in Tracey's grasp, dived for the corner where the rifle lay. Cursing a little, Tracey lurched forward, stamped down hard with his heel on the man's outstretched arm, heard his sharp intake of breath as the weight of his foot pinned the other to the floor.

'You heard what I said,' Tracey rasped. 'Now get to your feet and move out in front of me. Don't try any more tricks like that or I'll—'

He broke off at the sudden movement in the doorway of the shack, and the hard, anthoritative voice that said 'All right, Dillman. Back up.'

Tracey turned. The man who stood in the doorway held a gun trained on him. A second later, as the man stepped forward, his leather jacket folded back a little and he caught a brief glimpse of the star on the other's shirt. Behind him, standing a few feet outside the hut, he saw a handful of the men from the bar, and there was the farmer with them, his face bruised and bloodied, but the thin, sneering grin of triumph on his craggy features.

'You aiming to kill this man, Dillman?' snapped the other.

'I was goin' to take him with me to the military outpost, to get the Major there to have a talk with him,' said Tracey thinly.

'That is not true,' put in Indian Pete from the corner. He rubbed his wrist. 'He would have shot me in cold blood if you had not come when you did.'

'All right.' The other gave a brusque nod to Tracey. 'Step outside and keep your hands well away from those guns. We'll get to the bottom of this in due course and also what happened with that wagon trail you scouted for. I'm arrestin' you right now on a charge of suspected complicity with those outlaws.'

'Now you don't believe those foolish stories that have been goin' around,' protested Tracey. He kept his hands well away from his guns. 'They were started by this character here. The bartender in the saloon can verify that. He told me where I could locate this *hombre.*'

'Don't listen to the lyin' critter,' called the farmer from the background. 'He's just come back here looking for trouble. Tried to start somethin' in the saloon.'

'All right. You keep your mouth shut, Kearney. I'll see to this,' said the lawman. He motioned Tracey outside and as the other moved past him, his hand reached out and he jerked the Colts from Tracey's holsters, letting them drop on to the ground where one of the waiting deputies picked them up and thrust them into his own belt.

Tracey shrugged helplessly. There was nothing he could do at the moment. Unarmed, he could only do as this lawman said. He walked through the dust of the street, past the hotel where he had put up with a room, on to the jailhouse halfway along a side street. The Sheriff paused at the entrance to the office, turned to the men who had been following.

'All right, clear the street now, men. There's nothin' more to see here. The judge ought to be here in a week or ten days and we'll have the trial then.'

There was a little grumbling among the men, but they turned and made their way back along the street, only the farmer Tracey had beaten remaining where he stood with one foot up on the broadwalk. His eyes never left Tracey's face, even when the Sheriff snapped. 'I said there was nothing more to see, Kearney. Now on your way back to the saloon.'

The other's bruised and swollen lips parted in a vicious grin and there was something unholy at the back of his eyes. 'Just wanted to take one last look at this killer, Sheriff,' he said leeringly. 'Just make sure you keep him good and safe until the circuit judge gets here or we can get one from town. I want to be here when they sentence him and take him out to hang him. Even that'll be too good an end for the likes of him.'

'He ain't been found guilty yet, Kearney,' snapped the other, turning as the big farmer ambled off after the rest of the men.

Tracey went inside as the other gave him a push. They went through the small outer office, down a long passage to the rear of the building, stopping in front of one of the cells that opened out on to the central passage. Motioning him inside, the Sheriff locked the door behind him, stuffed the keys into his belt and stepped away.

'Better make yourself as comfortable as you can in there,' he said harshly. 'It's goin' to be where you'll stay for a little while. I'll get you some grub sent in from the hotel at meal times.'

'Thanks, Sheriff.' Tracey sat down on the edge of the low bunk set against the wall, listened to the other's footsteps receding into the distance. There was the hollow sound of another door closing at the far end of the passage and then silence. Getting to his feet, he tested the bars that were placed across the small square window in the cell, but they were set hard and firm into the opening and he knew there could be no escape that way.

Sitting back on the bunk, he tried to think things out. It had been a stupid thing to do to go out and look for Indian Pete. There had been the rest of the men still in the bar and they would have passed the word along to the

Sheriff that he was out to kill the other for talking about him in town. The Sheriff himself probably half-believed these rumours which had been started and it had not taken much to swing him around to these men's way of thinking. By now, he guessed dismally, Indian Pete would be on his way back along the trail west, to warn his outlaw friends that Tracey Dillman had discovered the link in New Orleans by means of which information was passed into the hills.

FIVE

Trial

It was on the ninth evening after he had been locked up in the jail that Tracey heard the trial was to be held in the courthouse the very next day. His supper had been brought to him and placed just inside the door of his cell by one of the deputies, but the other had said nothing when he had asked how long they intended to keep him there on this trumped-up charge and why they wouldn't allow him to get any word through to the Major at the outpost. Whether or not it would have done him any good if Major Allenton knew of his trouble, he did not know. Certainly he felt sure that the other did not believe he was in any way connected with these outlaws and had seriously considered his offer of help in rounding them up, had thought his anger sincere.

He ate his supper slowly, washing it down with the luke-warm coffee which the deputy had brought over from the hotel. Certainly it was clear that the town did not mean to spend too much money on food for its prisoners, especially one whom they believed had been responsible for the deaths of all those folk on that wagon train. He could-n't really blame these people for their obvious hatred towards him. These rumours had been started and nurtured for a definite reason. To get rid of him before he could cause any trouble. It was hardly surprising that the ordinary townsfolk believed them and once the seed of something like this was planted in a receptive and fertile mind, it would grow apace. There had to be some scapegoat here, close at hand, on whom to divert their anger and things had evidently been rigged so that he was the one.

He stood up and went over to the window, staring out through the iron bars into the darkening streets outside. The sun had gone down a long while before but there was the bright glow of the stars that hung endlessly in the heavens, glimmering along the foaming yeast of the universe, where the Milky Way spanned the wide arch of the heavens. A little stray breeze ran along the street now that the sun was down and the day's heat was fading swiftly. He felt it touch his forehead; cold on the sweat that had formed there. Inside the cell, during the full heat of the day, the atmosphere was like that of a vast oven, drawing all of the moisture in his body out through the pores of his flesh until it made him feel dried out inside.

In the distance, he could pick out the sound of raucous singing from one of the saloons, and occasionally, above the yelling voices, the tinkling of a piano and a richer sweeter voice than those that croaked and shouted at the tops of their lungs. The town was having itself a spree, he thought dully, and wondered at the reason for it. Maybe another paddle steamer had arrived at the levee and was disgorging its cargo, bringing goods and work to the town. Maybe another wagon train had arrived, was buying up stores from the warehouses along the waterfront.

There was a sudden movement at the end of the narrow alley that ran past the rear of the jailhouse. He turned his head sharply as his averted vision caught the faint movement. A shadow had slipped out from the main street into the alley and was sidling along the walls of the buildings to his right, moving in his direction. He felt a little thrill of expectancy, trying to figure out who it might be, intent on coming along to him unheard and unseen.

A few moments later, he was able to see the figure as the

man stood away from the wall. It was Kearney, the farmer he had whipped in the saloon. He felt his spirits sag a little.

'You in there, Dillman?' called the other in a soft tone.

Thinly, Tracey said: 'You know damned well I'm here, Kearney. Got something on your mind?'

'Just thought I'd let you know that Judge Winston arrived in town this afternoon. He's put up at the hotel now. They're holding your trial tomorrow and I figure by this time tomorrow evenin' you ought to be swingin' at the end of a rope.'

'You won't get that satisfaction, Kearney,' said Tracey grimly. 'Not even if you try to rig the jury.'

The other grinned, teeth showing in the dimness. 'Reckon we may do that, just to be on the safe side.'

He paused there for a long moment, looking in through the small window, then he spat on to the dusty alley, shuffled away without looking back. The night and the silence swallowed him up but Tracey knew that what the other had said had been no idle threat. The people of this town were determined that somebody should pay for the inhuman massacre of that wagon train, and they would do all in their power, legal or otherwise, to see that he paid the penalty. Only then would they be able to feel clean inside.

He went back to the bunk. A moment later, the deputy came back, picked up the plate and mug, went outside again, keeping an alert glance on Tracey, then locked the door behind him. He stood for a moment peering through the bars at the other, then said harshly: 'You'll be standin' trail tomorrow, mister.'

'I've already heard,' Tracey told him, sensing the surprise and bewilderment in the other.

'You joshin' me?' demanded the deputy thinly. He gripped on to the bars of the cell, forgetting for the moment that it was not part of his job to talk to any prisoner.

'Nope,' Tracey grinned. 'Had that farmer, Kearney

outside a minute or two back. Keen to tell me that I didn't
have a chance of being found innocent, that they would
rig the jury rather than allow that to happen.'

'Reckon you'd do better than listen to that kinda talk,'
growled the other. He seemed ill at ease as he stood there,
as if this news had somehow troubled him. 'You'll get a fair
trial, make no mistake about that.' He seemed on the
point of saying something further, then thought better of
it, spun on his heel and walked off carrying the eating
utensils in his left hand. The distant door closed dully and
silence came down on the jail. Tracey stretched himself
out on the bunk and pulled the single blanket over him.
The cot was hard and lumpy but he had somehow grown
used to it during the past eight nights and now he had no
difficulty in falling asleep, and even the thought of what
might be in store for him on the morrow did not keep him
awake.

The sunlight was pouring in through the small window
when he did finally awaken, with the hollow metallic
sound of the key grating in the lock of the cell door.
Stirring himself, he swung his legs to the floor and got up,
just as the Sheriff stepped inside. He laid the plate and
mug of coffee down on the floor close beside the bunk,
straightened, then stepped back. 'You heard about the
trial, Dillman?' he said. It was more of a statement than a
question, but the other gave a quick nod of his head.

'Sure, I heard about it last night,' he muttered. He
crammed some of the food into his mouth and chewed on
it slowly.

'There's been a lot of talk goin' around town durin' the
night that you're figuring on getting off this charge.'

Tracey glanced up, tried to probe the other's expression, but there was nothing there he could see that told
him of the thoughts the other was thinking at that
moment. 'What you're tryin' to say is that it don't matter
what I say, or how I try to defend myself, I'll be swingin' on
the end of the riata before sundown.'

'Now hold on there,' protested the other. 'I ain't sayin'

no such thing. But it don't matter what I think now. Soon as I deliver you to the courthouse, that'll be my part finished. It'll be up to the jury then to decide whether there's enough evidence against you or not.'

'I've already been given an idea of what sort of jury there'll be in that courthouse,' Tracey said bitterly. 'Seems like everybody in town has made up their minds about me and this trial is only a formality to make my hangin' all nice and legal, so that nobody will have anythin' on their conscience after it's over.'

The Sheriff said nothing to that, but he looked troubled as he turned away. When he came back half an hour later, to take Tracey over to the courtroom, the worried, apprehensive look was still on his face, even though he tried not to show it. He sat with Tracey in the front row, a little distance from the rest of the townsfolk who had managed to get in to see the trial. There were plenty more of them waiting outside the courthouse, Tracey had noticed.

Judge Winston came in a little while later, seated himself on the raised bench at the far end of the courtroom, looking out over the assembly below him. Once, only once, his glance flickered to Tracey, locked with his for a moment, then slid away again.

Tracey turned his attention to the jury. They looked a motley collection of men, taken from every walk of life to give a show of impartiality, he thought bitterly. They would probably find him guilty without having to retire to consider their verdict once this farce had played itself out to its inevitable conclusion.

The conversation at the rear of the room ceased as Judge Winston banged on the polished wood with his gavel, called the court to order. He said sternly: 'I understand that the charge brought against the prisoner is one of conspiracy with these outlaws who have been attacking the wagon trains moving west, killing and looting. This is a charge that calls for the death penalty and accordingly I shall give the prisoner every chance to defend himself.'

He spoke with a quiet dignity which dispelled any doubts that Tracey might have originally had as to the trustworthiness of this man. He was an upright and honest citizen, but no matter how honest he might be, there would be nothing that could be done if the jury found him guilty.

One after another, witnesses were called to testify that it was common knowledge that Tracey Dillman, the sole survivor of the wagon train disaster, had been in cahoots with the outlaws, supplying them with the information they needed in order to ambush the train, in return for which he had probably been paid well and what was more to the point, he was still alive, whereas all of the others had been killed.

Purely circumstantial evidence, but nevertheless, even Tracey was forced to admit when it had all been heard, that it made a bad case against him. Someone had been doing a lot of work getting all of this evidence built up against him while he had been recovering from that head wound at the military outpost. A lot of the evidence was deliberate fabrication, but it blended so well with the little half-truths that it was impossible to distinguish between false evidence and that which had been given in good faith by ordinary men and women who were merely retelling what had been told them.

He knew, deep inside, that no matter what he said in his own defence, it would not sway the jury. But he had to make the attempt.

'Do you wish to question any of the witnesses you've just heard?' asked Judge Winston as Tracey got to his feet.

'There's only one man I'd like to question,' Tracey said thinly. 'Indian Pete. He was the man I went to see to try to find out why these rumours were being spread around New Orleans. As the Sheriff can tell you, I was arrested on this trumped-up charge before I got around to questioning him properly. But I don't see him here in court today.' He turned his head and looked about him.

A moment later, there was a movement in the front row and Kearney pushed his huge bulk out of his seat. There was a faint sneer on his face as he said quietly: 'Indian Pete is a fur trapper, Judge. He comes into town every few weeks and then goes off again into the hills. He's somewhere in the hills now, I reckon. Ain't no way of getting word to him, I guess.'

'Is his evidence of vital importance to your defence?' asked the Judge, turning his glance to Tracey.

'I'm afraid so,' said the other. 'I believe that Indian Pete was the man who carried all of this information back to the outlaws, told them when a wagon train was moving out, how many men and rifles they carried, where they would take the trail out of the state and the best place to carry out an ambush. Those outlaws who attacked us, knew exactly where we would be and when. They couldn't have waited overlong in those rocks, certainly not more than a day or more, otherwise they would have been starving. I tell you, they knew we would be coming along and they knew how many men they would need. Even knew the kind of rifles we were carrying with us, the Spencer repeating rifles.'

'Those outlaws knew that all right because you told 'em. Maybe when you went scouting ahead you had a parley with 'em,' roared Kearney.

'Silence,' called Judge Winston. 'This court will be conducted in the proper way or I shall have everyone cleared.'

Kearney sank back in his chair, silenced by what the other said, but he had made his point, and it had been noted by the jury as something additional to use against Tracey when they came to deliver their verdict.

'Do you have any proof that this man was guilty?' asked Judge Winston, leaning forward to peer down at Tracey.

'I could have got the proof from him,' said the other harshly, 'If I had been given the chance to make him talk.'

'But at the moment you cannot substantiate what you say?'

'No.' Tracey shook his head. Inwardly, he doubted what Kearney had said. He felt certain that Indian Pete had now outlived his usefulness to these outlaws and was either dead, or being held prisoner somewhere where he could give them no further trouble.

'I see. And do you wish to call anyone else to testify for your defence?' It was a purely superfluous question, Tracey reflected wearily. 'There is no one else,' he said thinly, speaking through tightly clenched teeth. 'All of those who could have testified in my defence were killed by those murderin' outlaws in the hills.'

There was a loud, raucous laugh from Kearney, silenced quickly as Judge Winston swung on him sharply. A moment later, the other said: 'The details in this case are reasonably plain. There is evidence against the man accused, but all of this is circumstantial. No one has yet testified as to having seen him give any of this information to any of the outlaws. It has been supposed that he could have done this when riding scout for the wagon train, while he claims that he always rode with another scout named Denton. As the witnesses have pointed out, Denton is no longer alive and cannot give evidence. We are there-fore left in the unenviable position of having no direct evidence for either accusing this man, or in his own defence. It will be up to the jury to decide whether he is guilty or innocent.' He turned to face the men on the long bench. 'If you wish, you may leave the room to talk over what you've heard and then give your verdict or—'

'We don't reckon there's any need for that, Judge.' The tall, black-bearded man at the end of the bench got to his feet. He stared directly at Tracey as he spoke. 'We've heard enough here for us to make up our minds about this *hombre*. He's guilty all right.'

Tracey felt the muscles of his stomach tighten convul-sively at the other's words and even though the verdict had been expected, they came with the shock of the unex-pected. He stood perfectly still, felt the little trickle of sweat form on his forehead and begin to run down the side of his face.

He hoped that the look of fear did not show through

on his features. To die this way was something he had never contemplated before. In a gunfight, maybe, for that came to many men who lived the sort of life he did. But not at the end of a rope.

He grew aware that Judge Winston was glancing in his direction. He thought from the other's expression that he did not agree with this verdict, and it came to Tracey that perhaps he too had realized now that this was a rigged jury, that he would have been found guilty no matter how he had defended himself; that it was a foregone conclusion and had only needed the Judge himself to be present to give it a look of being legal.

He saw Winston open his mouth to say something, noticed in that same glance the look of undisguised hatred and triumph on Kearney's face. Then there came a sudden interruption at the back of the courthouse. There was the sound of an angry voice which seemed vaguely familiar and then he saw the erect figure that pushed its way through the crowd of men near the doorway and strode into the middle of the courtroom.

'I think this farce has gone on just a little too long,' Major Allenton glared around him a little before fixing his attention on the men of the jury. 'This man is completely innocent of this charge which has been brought against him. And unless the men of this rigged jury want me to look a little more closely into their reasons for giving this verdict, I would advise them to leave right away.'

Scarcely were the words out of his mouth, then there was a hurried movement on the long bench, as the men almost fell over themselves to get out of the courtroom. Major Allenton did not give them a second glance, apparently confident that his order would be obeyed without question. He walked over to Judge Winston, said something to him in a low undertone, then came back to where Tracey stood, still scarcely able to comprehend what was happening. It was as if he were somewhere else, watching these proceedings through eyes which were not his own, watching himself standing there.

'Seems to me I got here just in time,' said the Major briskly. He did not look at the Sheriff. 'You'll be coming back with me.'

Tracey nodded, stepped out of the well of the court. No one made any move to stop him. Outside, there was a handful of soldiers in uniform, rifles at the ready, but there was no need for them to have to use their weapons. It was just possible, Tracey thought, that most of the ordinary men and women were now convinced of his innocence, were aware that he was being accused so that the real criminals went free.

'How come you did turn up then?' asked Tracey, as they walked along the street for a little way to where the horses were tethered.

'It wasn't by accident,' said the other grimly. 'We were riding in this direction when I heard that you had been arrested for this crime. A couple of days ago we found the body of a man on the trail about fifteen miles out of town. One of my men recognized it as that of Indian Pete, an old trapper who often frequented the post, then went off for long stretches into the hills. He's been shot in the back.'

'I figured they'd have to do something like that,' Tracey said slowly. 'He knew a little too much and he could have talked.'

'That's right,' Allenton nodded tersely. 'We've got 'em scared, but that isn't enough. Scared men sometimes make mistakes and until they do, we're no closer to finding their hideout than we were when you first came into the outpost.'

They saddled up. A horse had been got from somewhere for Tracey and he pulled himself up easily into the saddle. In front of them, the main street leading west was quiet and empty, but with little eddies of dust still hanging in the air, indicating to anyone who knew how to read the sign, that a rider had lit out of town in a big hurry only a little while before, while they had been inside the courthouse. As they reached the edge of town, cut up into the low land that lay on the fringe of New Orleans, Tracey smelt the sharpness of the dust again in his nostrils. He turned to the Major.

'A rider left town shortly before we did and headed out this way in a mighty big hurry. Reckon it could have been somebody headin' west to warn those hombres in the hills that their plan didn't work and I'm still around.'

Major Allenton nodded. 'I'd noticed that,' he said slowly. He stared off thoughtfully into the distance. 'It could mean that they may try to stop you again. It's possible we could turn this to our advantage. Are you prepared to act as decoy for us, so that we can bait a trap for these men?'

Tracey grinned mirthlessly. 'Seems to me that I've been baiting a trap for a long time now, Major, and it hasn't got us anywhere, except for getting me almost hanged back yonder. Reckon if I was to ride back there sometime, they may even try to pin that same charge on me again.'

'Not if we can round up this bunch of cold-blooded murderers,' said the other with a deceptive mildness.

They rode west, through the low lying land, across a wide river with marsh on either bank and then up into the hills. The high noon sun lay with a heavy, stifling pressure on them as they rode in single file, with Tracey riding immediately behind the Major. They kept to the trail, occasionally passing a wooden cabin built back from the trail, set well into the timber, as though the man who had built it had not wanted any unwelcome curiosity from anyone riding by. There were many men in these hills, men on the run from the law, or from a host of other things which hounded them all their lives. Tracey had known from past experience that most of these men were of no danger to anyone provided they were left strictly alone. They were not the same breed of men as those vicious gunwolves who inhabited the hills further west, preying on others, killing and robbing whenever the opportunity arose.

The trail began a gradual ascent into red fir lands, where the tall trees lifted clear and high against the undulating skyline of the hills. By late afternoon, the land had become mottled with shadow, shade and sunlight lying over everything in a shimmering of heat. It was a three day ride out to the military post and that evening, as dusk was darkening the sky, turning the world into a metal blue land, touching everything with that bloom one got on the barrel of a new rifle, they made camp in a wide hollow a hundred yards or so off the trail.

As they ate around the fire, Tracey asked the Major: 'Back in the courtroom this morning, you said I could help you.'

The other nodded, chewed on a strip of beef for a moment, then swilled it down with coffee. 'Three weeks ago, we had a man at the outpost talking about a new rifle he claimed they were designing. I might have mentioned it to you when you were there. I'd like you to meet him when he comes back again, in a week's time. He's been in Washington, hoping to interest the Government in it. Could be that this is the weapon we've all been waiting for.'

'And how can I help?'

'We'll talk about that when we get back to camp,' said the other firmly. The night closed in around them and there was only the flickering red glow of the fire lighting the trees around the clearing.

The next day, they continued the ride north-west, turning from the main wagon trail that led on until it hit the Alkali Flats. Their trail led off from this, heading more to the north, into the thick timber, cutting across the rivers closer to their sources, so that they were running faster and deeper, though narrower here than lower down where Tracey remembered crossing them the last time he had ridden in this direction. For a long moment, the memory of those men and women who had made that last fateful journey with him was strong in his mind and he felt the coldness of his spine and his fingers tighten convulsively on the leather of the reins. He felt shocked by sudden depth of his feeling, had not realized that it still affected him so greatly. He fell to wondering what sort of men this Carrico and Laredo were, utterly ruthless, letting nothing stand in their way and thinking nothing whatever of taking life. Half of those men and women in the train must have been unarmed when the outlaws had swept down and finished them off, he thought with a faint sense of shock.

Through the forest's endless quiet, they rode, hooves muffled by the thick carpet of needles and leaves. They saw no one else along the trail although Tracey had the feeling that the forest was not deserted. Occasionally, he thought he heard vague, tag-ends of sound filtering through the dense tree growth, but he could not be sure.

The edge went off Tracey's uneasiness as they neared the outpost. He wasn't sure yet what was in the Major's mind, but the other seemed to have formulated some plan. Now that Indian Pete was dead, shot down by the men he had trusted, they would need some other means of getting their information from New Orleans. By mid-afternoon, they were moving out of the timber, along a winding trail that led across rougher country, filled with narrow gullies and canyons, pocked here and there by upthrusting rocks fluted and etched into strange, fantastic shapes by the wind. This was territory that lay on the edge of the Badlands a little further to the south, he reckoned. It would be a regular morass when it rained, but for close on ten months of the year, there would be no rain, and the trail was ankle deep in white dust that lifted under the hooves of their horses and hung in the air like a cloud, getting into their eyes and nostrils, blinding and choking. Even with the coming of evening, as they rode more slowly, the terrain looked grim and forbidding.

He shielded his face and lit the cigarette which he had rolled a few moments before. Far off to the west, the sky held a curiously dark haze where a blanket of deepening grey was moving rapidly over the heavens. The sun was rapidly blotted out before it could touch the hills and he guessed that the long period of drought was due to come to an end pretty soon. There was a storm brewing over the far hills, moving rapidly in their direction. He shivered a little. They would undoubtedly sleep wet that night, but fortunately, with any luck it should be the last night on the trail. By that time the next day they ought to have reached the outpost.

A brilliant fork-tongued flash lit the horizon directly ahead of them. He blinked his eyes against it, heard the dull, low rumble of thunder. Around them now, there was no projecting ledge where they might camp in the lee of some hill, out of the worst of the rain. The ground was as flat as a table except for the narrow gullies that slashed across it. Shrugging in resignation, he spurred his mount forward a little as the Major yelled a sharp command, waving the troops forward.

The stillness of the air which had heralded the approach of the storm was suddenly broken. Wind rushed at them across the flatness of the plateau, struck them forcibly in their saddles. The first raindrops fell heavily on their faces, pocked the dust around them where it flowed like a river to the very edge of the trail, whipping up into writhing whorls of grey as the wind caught it. But these lifting eddies were brief things, flattened instantly it seemed as the downpour struck. It came without warning, within seconds, that teeming torrent which hit them from the west. Thudding hooves could just be heard as thunder rode with them. Darkness came in a swift swoop. There was no dimming twilight this night. The sun was gone and the storm veered overhead, beserk clouds racing on, sending the rain driving down at them.

There was a strange almost beautiful savagery in the scene around them as Nature showed them in the raw what mighty forces she could use if she really put her mind to it, showing them in no uncertain manner how puny men really were when it came to the point. Lightning forked and cracked overhead and in every lightning stroke, it was possible to glimpse the millions of brilliant raindrops, as if they had been caught and frozen into immobility by the searing flash.

Tracey pushed his sight through the darkness, riding close in line with the rest of the men, looking as they went for a place to make camp, any place where they might find some shelter from the rain which struck at them in a seemingly solid sheet of water.

Half an hour passed. Drenched to the skin, their clothing clinging to their legs and bodies, flesh numbed by the continual rain, ears deafened by the rolling thunder, and eyes strained by the incessant flashing of the lightning, they rode along a trail that twisted and wound in every direction. There were times when Tracey felt sure they were lost, that the Major was not sure of which direction they were moving in.

Then, slowly, imperceptibly at first, the roar of the thunder began to lessen, to pass away with the flashing lightning, moving towards the eastern horizon as the trailing edge of the storm moved over them. In the west, it was just possible to see the bright sparks of a few stars low down, close to the skyline and a little while later, there was a definite clear stretch there, widening every minute as the cloud wrack passed overhead and continued to move away east.

A cold wind followed in the trail of the storm and soon they were shivering in their saddles, heads bowed as they leaned forward, content now to let their mounts pick their way forward at their own pace.

An hour passed in the cold night. It was obvious, thought Tracey, that the Major knew this territory like the back of his hand, knew where there was a fine camping ground. If the country was all like this, it would not matter how far they rode that night and they might just as well have stopped and made camp where they were rather than continuing to ride in its discomfort. Ten minutes later, the trail swung sharply right, they rode down between the rearing walls of a deep canyon, out into the open once more and Tracey saw, as he had begun to suspect, that the

country here was less open and rough, there was a smat-
tering of mesquite and scrub oak, and then larger bushes
and finally a thin edge of timber that lifted along the side
of a wide ridge on to which they rode after climbing
steeply from the canyon trail which, as far as he could see
in the faint glimmering glow of starlight, continued on
ahead of them across open country.

There was soon a fire going and bacon and beans heat-
ing over it, with the pleasant aroma of hot coffee in the air.
The men gradually forgot some of the discomfort of their
wet clothing and the storm they had just ridden through,
as they seated themselves around the blaze, eating the
food which had been prepared. The horses were hobbled
off in the brush and there was no chance of them straying
through the night.

Wrapped in his blankets, Tracey stared up at the bright,
starlit sky over his head, still turning events over in his
mind as he had the past two nights. He wondered about
this new type of rifle which Major Allenton had talked
about. Was it really the weapon they needed so desperately
here on the frontier? It was an easy thing for a man like
him, living close to this wild, untamed country, to visualize
just how big a part such a weapon could play in the opening up of the territory.

There was a tremendous need for further expansion
westward, away from the densely crowded land along the
eastern side of the continent. The exodus had begun, in a
small way, before the war, but now it would gain impetus,
become the biggest movement of humanity since the
Israelites left Egypt. There was a rich land full of promise
on the western seaboard of America. Red gold had been
found there, but there was need for more people to move
in that direction, across the vast uncharted wilderness
which lay between. There were many dangers on the way;
everyone realized that, but they would be overcome in
time, he felt sure. If only they could get the wagon trains
moving and be able to protect them against the outlaws
and Indians who still wandered this territory. The Indians

couldn't be blamed for their activities. They were merely defending country which had been theirs for centuries and which they regarded as sacred. But the outlaws were different; vicious, savage killers, who plundered simply for money, men on the run from the law, shunned by society, outcasts who lived only for death and destruction.

The next day, at noon, they rode into the compound of the outpost. While the men of the troop went to to their quarters, Tracey followed the Major into his quarters. The other waved him to a chair, then seated himself behind the desk. For a long moment, the Major sat there, his face intent, as if he were listening to something just at the limit of audibility.

When the other made no move to speak, Tracey said: 'You told me on the way here that you had some plan in mind, Major.'

Allenton seemed to stir himself with an effort, as if becoming aware of the other's presence in the room with him for the first time. Then he nodded his head briskly.

'That's right, Dillman. In a little while, I'll take you over to the armoury and show you one of the new Winchester rifles. See what you think of it, whether it can help us.'

'And then what do I do?'

The other sat up straight in his chair, the iron-grey hair glistening a little in the sunlight streaming through the window at his back. 'The way I see it, these outlaws will be getting more information from New Orleans and the other jumping-off places for the wagon trains. They killed Indian Pete, the man who gave them most of the news from New Orleans, but make no mistake about it, they will have someone else there by now, ready to pass the word along whenever another train is ready to go.

'I want you to join one of these trains, sign on as scout again. It may not be easy. Even though I'm damned sure of your innocence, and most of the other folk in New Orleans probably are too, you've made yourself a reputation and it won't be easy to fight that.'

'Whatever happens, I want to go on through to

California,' Tracey said simply. 'That's where I was headed with that other train when we were jumped on the state borders.'

'Maybe you'll get your wish this way,' declared the other, lighting a cigar. 'All I'm interested in at the moment is this outlaw band which is operating out there. We'll have to play this carefully. They have too many spies around for us to take any chances. But once you've got yourself fixed up with one of these trains, I'll have some of my men put with it. If I was to send a troop of soldiers along with you, they'd be spotted twenty or thirty miles away and the outlaws would fade into the hills before we got near them.'

'That makes sense,' Tracey admitted.

'Sure it makes sense.' The other lifted his voice a little, lips clamped around the cigar, puffing at it furiously. 'I've been trying to get Washington to see the difficulties I've got to face out here but they refuse to accept any of the despatches I send them as urgent. They reckon that every other commander along this god-forsaken frontier is in the same position and they don't have the men to send everywhere, so they had to have some priority, and we're one hell of a way down the list.' He raised one hand and rubbed at his forehead where his cap had rubbed a raw, red mark in the flesh. His hand dropped and he sat motionless at the desk again.

For a long moment, he sat there staring in front of him, as if trying to rationalise within himself, in his own thoughts, why he had been left to try to fight this war against Indians and outlaws with less than half the number of men he so obviously needed.

Finally, he pushed back his chair, got to his feet. 'Let's take a walk over to the armoury,' he suggested, putting on his cap once more, tugging it down firmly on his head. They went out into the heat of the dusty compound. Horses were tethered in a long line to a hitching rope stretched between a couple of posts. A little further away, men were drilling and others, under a man with Sergeant's stripes on his arm, were riding their mounts around the wide courtyard, learning to ride them like the Apaches, so that horse and rider became as one.

The Corporal Tracey had met earlier was there in the armoury. He gave him a quick nod of greeting, then went back to his work, realizing that the watchful eye of the Major was on him. There was another man there, a stranger to Tracey, a civilian with a sharp, though likeable face and quick, alert eyes that passed over the other's face, missing nothing, quiet and appraising.

'This is Willard Thorpe,' said Major Allenton, introducing the other to Tracey. 'He brought up some of the new rifles, the Winchesters.'

Tracey shook hands with the other, then almost at once, he forgot the man as a bright-shining gun was pushed into his hands and he turned it over and over slowly, examining it from every angle; and he knew almost at once, deep inside him, that this was the rifle they had been waiting for, that with a weapon like this they could defeat anything they might run up against on this untamed, wild frontier of theirs.

'The action of reloading and cocking the hammer is purely automatic,' said Thorpe, demonstrating the action to him. 'One simply has to use this finger lever, with the cartridges in the stock of the rifle and one can fire without taking the gun from its position.'

'Meaning that you don't have to take aim again each time you fire,' said Major Allenton.

'With these, we can push through to California and nothing could stop us,' he said definitely. He looked across at Thorpe. 'Give us these guns and we'll open up the frontier for you.'

'They'll be coming along soon,' promised the other, nodding his head. 'As yet, we have only a few of them. As you'll realize, it is essential that they should not fall into the wrong hands or that could be disastrous.'

Tracey checked the loading action for himself, marvelling at the ease and rapidity with which it could be operated. There was none of the stiffness he had found with the Spencer or Henry rifles. With a rifle like this it would be able to pick off six men while the enemy were firing one shot in return. He handed the rifle back towards Thorpe, but the other shook his head slightly, a faint smile on his lips. He pushed the gun back at him.

'No, Dillman,' he said softly. 'That is your rifle.'

For a moment, there was astonishment in Tracey's mind. He knew that his fingers were curled around the stock and barrel of the gun, gripping it tightly, as if afraid to let it go. He was aware of the Major looking at him, standing tautly erect.

'That's right,' said Allenton, after a brief pause. 'I said I wanted you to help me in this spot of trouble we have here. You'll need a gun to do that and I figure that this is the best rifle we have.'

'I don't know what to say.' For the first time in his life, Tracey felt at a complete loss for words. He felt full of emotion, struggling to say what was really in his mind. Then he held the rifle loosely in his right hand, faced the Major. 'With this gun, we can bring those outlaws to justice, I'm sure, sir,' he said.

Allenton nodded briskly. 'There'll be more wagon trains moving out within the next few weeks and with luck you ought to be able to sign on with one of them as scout. They won't find it easy to get good men and you may come across one wagon master who doesn't heed these stories that have been going around. I'll have one of my men in New Orleans waiting to hear from you and then we'll put that plan of ours into operation. I can't order you to do any of this, you know that, but knowing how you feel about the shooting of those others in that wagon train, I don't think you're the kind of man to back out now that the going is likely to get tough.'

Tracey nodded. He could feel the weight of the rifle in his hands and it gave him a kind of reassurance that he had not felt for a long while. Now they had a good chance of ridding the borders of this gang that had been ambushing the wagon trains time after time. When that was done, not only would he have been vindicated and cleared of any complicity with these outlaws, but the trail west would be that little bit safer than before and it would encourage more settlers to move out. It would not remove all of the danger; it would be years before they succeeded in that, if they ever did manage it.

He spent the next day with Thorpe, learning everything there was to know about the new Winchester. There were several now on the outpost and it would not be long before every company was issued with them, and then they would be sold to the frontiersmen, the scouts and settlers. Very soon, it would become the favoured weapon of the frontier. How long it would hold that position unchallenged he did not know, but from the looks of it, and the way it handled, he could not see anything seriously challenging it for a long while to come.

Next morning, as soon as it was light, he left the outpost, heading back to the east, along the trail he had travelled with Major Allenton and his troops a few days before. Riding alone, he expected to make better time than before, hoping to be back in New Orleans within a couple of days. The Winchester now reposed in the scabbard of his saddle and he wore the twin Colts in their holsters, tied low, ready for trouble. Now that he had been cleared by the Major, back in that New Orleans courtroom, he did not intend to take any further bucking from anyone there, and that included the Sheriff. He reached the timber by mid-day, paused for a while in its shade, the sharp scent of pine needles in his nostrils, eating a little of the dried venison he had brought with him. He did not bother to build a fire, but let the horse graze on the short grass that grew among the trees, widely spaced at this point, while he lit a smoke, lying back on the soft ground, listening with part of his mind for any sound of other riders in the vicinity, but hearing nothing.

He rode on through the heat of the long afternoon, along a trail that was well used and broad, winding in and out of the trees. He pushed his horse most of the way, anxious to get as much of the distance covered as possible, only occasionally slowing to a walk, giving his horse a breathing spell, hating the delay so that he could scarcely abide it, the restlessness bubbling up in his mind, tightening his teeth in his mouth, lumping the muscles of his cheeks and jaw under the tanned skin. Deep inside, the thought of what had happened in that narrow valley continued to dominate him, almost to the exclusion of everything else. There was really nothing else left in him but this desire to even the score, to wipe out the memory of that evening in blood. It had been something that had changed his life, it had changed his mind and heart more than anything else he had experienced. Even the war had not done that to him, for in the war he had been fighting men who had had the same chance of survival as he himself, men armed as he was with similar weapons. He had not figured that his chance for revenge would have come as quickly as this, nor that he would have the means to carry it through.

He reached a flat stretch of country and set his horse forward at a steady canter in the growing dimness. The air blew cool against his face and at his back, the sun was almost down, the redness fading as the deep purple hush of the coming night descended on the land. He rode for another two hours, until he felt the tall columns of rock on either side of him begin to push their shoulders out towards the trail, crowding in on it from either side, crushing the track until it was nothing more than a narrow ribbon, a grey scar in the darkness, which he could only just make out. Creeks ran down the sides of the steep slopes, and the sound of rushing wate, bubbling over loose stones was now in his ears, at the same time as he smelled the damp air that always lifted from these narrow watercourses. He was high up now, after riding out of the tall timber earlier that evening and he had the strange feeling that the whole weight of the terrain about him had slipped to one side, shifting eastward away from the trail as the tall hills lifted in dull shadow against the sky, blotting out the bright stars which shone in the deep yeasty depths of the universe's firmament high over his head.

Even though the air now blew with an increasing coldness against him, he continued to ride, knowing that he would make cold camp when he did force himself to halt. There would be no sense in lighting a fire here. It would be seen for several miles and unlike the previous occasion, there were no soldiers around now to pitch in and help if he was discovered and attacked by anyone watching this trail back to New Orleans.

Around the bend in the trail, he caught a glimpse of a huddled cluster of darker shadows just a little distance below him and he strained his sight to distinguish them from their background, trying to make out what they were, slowing his mount to see better in the darkness.

Turning, he found a trail that led away to his right in the direction of the shadows and as he approached, he saw that they were a huddle of old shacks split by the narrow trail which went straightaway through them, cleaving the little mining place in twain. Beside the township, he was able to make out the ugly scars in the hillside where the mining operations had been carried out, but by the look of the place, it had been abandoned and deserted many years before.

Nevertheless, he approached the place warily, eyes alert for the faintest movement in the deep midnight shadows that lay among the huts. His hand hung a few inches above the Colt in his holster, ready to snake down and draw within seconds if there was any danger here. But there was no sound, no movement. As he had suspected, the place had been abandoned sometime in the past ten or twenty years, possibly because the gold or silver vein had run out, possibly because of sickness there, or even the war. Then he went closer to the nearest shack and discovered the real reason why it had been deserted.

The arrows were still embedded in the thick wood of the doorposts and around the small windows, telling their own grim tale of an Indian attack on this tiny settlement.

Such incidents had been common ten years back. The Indians here often considered these mountains and hills as sacred, the resting places of their gods and spirits, and they fought and killed anyone who went into them. The miners here had paid dearly for their attempts to win precious metal from the hills and streams.

But their misfortune was his good luck. At least, he would sleep dry and reasonably warm tonight, in more comfort than he had been anticipating. He tethered the horse in front of one of the shacks, then made his way inside. The musty smell of the abandoned place greeted him, stinging the back of his nostrils and dust lifted under his feet where it had lain undisturbed since the massacre of the camp's inhabitants. Something shifted and scuttled away in one corner and he whirled instinctively. A snake – or a rat? He caught a glimpse of the red eyes that glared balefully at him from the dimness. Rats he could tolerate, he thought as he pulled his blanket from the saddle roll, preparing to bed down for the night. Snakes were a different proposition. In the morning, he would continue his journey to New Orleans, probably reaching the town before nightfall.

SIX

Hired Scout

Tracey smelled the coffee and roasting meat before he came in sight of the small group of wagons, clustered together as if for warmth on the very edge of New Orleans. Here, they were away from the houses and stores, out in the beginnings of open country. Most of the townsfolk did not like the wagon trains meeting inside the town itself and by this time, they were being forced to congregate outside the limits of the town. It meant they had to go a little further for their supplies, but nobody seemed to be minding that.

For the past seven weeks, Tracey had been moving from one wagon train to another, seeking a job with them, but on every occasion, he had been refused when someone had recognized him. Whether or not they really believed the stories they had heard, or they were just not going to take any chances on them being true, it was difficult to tell, but he was beginning to despair of ever getting a job as scout with one of them. The thought at the back of his mind now was that if he failed again, he would simply forget what Major Allenton had told him, and would ride out himself, into those wide and lonely hills and track down the outlaws by himself.

His belly contracted a little as the smell of beef and beans hit him. Touching spurs to his mount, he rode forward, pausing as he came to the edge of the ring of wagons. Everywhere he could see, there was intense activity; men lifting the heavy casks of meat and salt into the backs of the wagons, toting the barrels of water into place, strapping them carefully in position by the long, leather straps which hung from the back of the Conestogas. The women were busy too, getting the supplies on board, stacking everything they would need into the backs of the wagons. Even the children seemed to be helping, Tracey noticed.

As he sat there, eyeing the scene, he heard a heavy drawling voice at his back. 'You gettin' an eyeful of everythin', mister?'

He stiffened in the saddle, feeling his muscles grow taut under his jacket. His pulses raced a little although he doubted if there was anything for him to be afraid of, but the tone had been distinctly unfriendly. Slowly, keeping his hands well clear of his guns, he wheeled his mount, turning to face the other. He had not heard the other soft-footing it up behind him and cursed himself for his lack of attention. One mistake like that could cost him his life, he told himself with a fierce savagery.

The man who sat easily in the saddle eyeing him up and down with a sneering insolent look was thick-set, broad-shouldered, with several days' growth of black beard on his slab-like features, as if he were trying to grow a beard and moustache and not having much luck with it at the moment.

'I asked you a question, mister,' he said again, his voice thick and hoarse.

Reaching up, Tracey rubbed the back of his hand over his forehead to wipe away a little of the sweat which had formed there. He said casually, too casually, 'I smelled the grub and rode over to take a look-see,' he replied. 'You startin' to head out west?'

'That's right,' grunted the other. He nodded his head ponderously. His eyes narrowed a little in speculative concentration. 'Ain't I seen your face somewhere before?'

Tracey tightened his lips, shook his head. 'We've never

met before,' he said positively. He did not recognize the other, had not seen him before in his life.

'I'm sure I know you.' The other was evidently trying hard to recall where he had seen Tracey's face before, then he gave up the attempt, said coarsely: 'If you've seen enough then, mister, I reckon you'd better mosey along. We ain't partial to strangers hanging around the wagons, particularly when we don't know who they are.'

'I was wonderin' if there might be a job,' Tracey said casually. 'You seem to have plenty of wagons here. Might need a scout.'

'We don't need anybody,' retorted the other harshly. He edged his mount forward until he had ridden up alongside Tracey, leaning over in his saddle. to thrust his face up to the other's. 'Now ride on, mister. We've got no place for you in the train.'

'You the wagon master here?'

'No. But I've got a say in whether or not we need anybody with us.'

Tracey grinned easily. 'I like to get my walking papers from the boss of the outfit,' he said quietly.

He saw the deep flush that spread up swiftly from the other's bull-like neck, suffusing his face, heightening his colour. He sucked in a deep breath and his ham-like fist clenched on the pommel of his saddle. 'You lookin' for trouble around here, mister?' he asked tautly.

'I don't aim to start any,' Tracey said, eyeing the other, measuring him, recognizing instantly the type of man he was, a bully and a braggart, possibly thinking himself something of a gunman, knowing that he could handle himself in a rough-and-tumble fight, especially with a man a lot lighter than himself. But something in the hard, agate-still eyes that watched him, made him pause. Tracey went on slowly, 'But I figure that if anybody does start something, I aim to finish it.'

For a second, the other's glance lowered to the guns worn low, then flickered to the rifle in the scabbard and his eyes widened just a shade. He sucked in his lips, seemed on the point of saying something further, when a man came striding from the centre of the circle of wagons.

'All right, all right, there'll be no trouble here,' said the other in a deep, authoritative tone. He eyed Tracey closely, lips held together. 'I'll handle this, Blaine.'

'Suit yourself,' muttered the other, eyeing Tracey darkly, with a look that promised more trouble if the two ever met again. 'But he isn't the kind of man for you, Mister Everett. He's a saddle-bum on the loose from some posse if I ever saw one. He'll throw in his lot with you, just to stay one jump ahead of the law and he'll always be throwing a look over his shoulder, clear to California.'

'I like to hear a man speak up for himself,' said the other firmly. 'I gave most of you that chance when you came askin' for a job with the train. I can only do the same for him.'

Blaine shrugged broad shoulders, half turned. He still seemed intent on arguing the point with the other in spite of the fact that, as Tracey had already gathered, this man in front of him was the real wagon boss here, the man who gave the orders, and who said who was hired.

'Don't let him talk you into anythin' though. Remember that there's a heap of miles of bad country between us and California. We've got to cross it before we get to safety and I'd like to know every man I'm ridin' with, know who I can trust and who I have to watch. We can't be too careful and I reckon I've seen this man's face somewhere before – could have been on some wanted poster back east a stretch.'

'Very likely your picture would be alongside mine,' retorted Tracey, feeling some of the hot anger boiling up inside him at the other's remark. With an effort, he forced the anger down, kept it under rigid control. The big man muttered something unintelligible under his breath, then pulled hard on the reins and rode off towards the camp, easing his mount between two of the wagons, pausing only to yell something at one of the men there, venting his anger on the first person to cross his path.

Tracey followed him for a moment with his narrowed gaze and then turned back to the other. The man who stood in front of him, his feet planted well apart was tall and thin-faced, his complexion almost as darkly tanned as Tracey's. His eyes were a deep and vivid blue, frank and open.

'You seem ready to jump down anybody's throat,' he said after a brief pause. 'You're not on the run from the law, are you?'

Tracey shook his head. 'No,' he said slowly. 'All I want to do is to get to California. There's nothing for a man here since the war. The carpetbaggers from the North are coming down and takin' everything they can lay their hands on, whether they leave us bare or not. I want to get to a new land where a man can make somethin' of himself and start to put down his roots with his own land on which to build something permanent.'

'Well, I figure you'll find that out in California, if we ever get there,' went on the other seriously. He came forward, motioned Tracey down from his mount. 'But I figure that the first thing as far as you're concerned, is some grub. Better light down and come on into the camp. We can talk things over better there.'

He led the way between two of the wagons, into the clearing where two fires had been hit. Tracey sat cross-legged and took the plate which one of the women held out to him with a faint, shy smile. He ate hungrily, feeling ravenous, washing down the excellent meal with the coffee that was poured into his cup until he could swallow no more. Then the man seated near him said: 'Permit me to introduce myself. Grant Roberts is the name. As you can see, we're headin' for California in a couple of days just as soon as we get everythin' loaded into the wagons.' His gaze lifted. 'You know anythin' of this country?'

'Some,' Tracey nodded. 'I've been west for maybe fifty miles or more.' He did not want to talk overmuch about that last wagon train, could guess at the feelings this would evoke if the other knew about that episode.

'You could be a big help to us,' nodded the other, inwardly digesting that piece of information.

Tracey opened his mouth to say something further but at that precise moment there was an interruption. Glancing round, he saw Blaine advancing on them from the direction of one of the wagons. There was a sneering look of triumph on the man's broad features. He came right up to them, then said through clenched teeth. 'I thought I knew you, mister.' His voice was gritty and harsh. He turned to Roberts. 'You know who this man is, Roberts?'

'No,' murmured the other, his brows knit into a straight line. 'Though I fail to see what that has got to do with you.'

'He's one of them pesky outlaws,' snarled the other. I thought I'd seen his face before. This is that *hombre*, Dillman, they arrested here a little while ago and tried for being in cahoots with those killers who ambushed that last train out of New Orleans. He sold them down the river. Acted as scout for the train and then left them when those outlaws hit 'em somewhere west of here.'

For a moment, there was a rough hardness to Roberts's face. He made to say something, then bit it back with an effort, laid his stern and severe gaze on Tracey.

'Your name is Dillman?' he said. It was more of a statement than a question.

'That's right,' declared Tracey tightly. He lifted his gaze to the big man standing over him. 'But this *hombre* lies in his teeth when he says I was in cahoots with those killers. I was tried and shown to be innocent by Major Allenton, in command of the outpost three days' ride from here. Even though the jury was rigged to find me guilty, it didn't work.'

'You're as guilty as hell and everybody in town knows it,' snarled Blaine. His eyes were narrowed in his head, lips drawn back in a snarling grin. 'That Major had no call to drag you out of that courthouse and force 'em to set you free. I figure that maybe some of the folk in town might like to know where you are. Wouldn't take 'em long to rustle up a posse and come ridin' for you. This time they won't wait for a trail, they'll simply ride you out and string you up from the nearest branch.'

'This time, I'll make sure they don't take me,' Tracey said throatily. 'You seem to forget that Indian Pete was shot in the back along the trail to stop him from tellin' the truth, and I was locked away in that jail when that happened.'

For a moment, the other seemed at a temporary loss for words. Tracey could see from his expression that he had scored there, that the man had no answer for that. Then the other muttered harshly: 'I still say you were guilty and I for one don't aim to ride with a man like you.'

His expression was ugly. He was obviously looking for trouble, wanting to start and finish this thing there, at that moment. Tracey remained seated, though not once taking his attention off the other, alert for any sudden move he might try to make.

'Quiet, both of you,' snapped Roberts. He got to his feet. 'I've heard about you, Dillman. What I've heard has all been against you. They say in town that you have a reputation for being fast with a gun, that you fought with the South in the war, although I don't hold that against any man. But from what I have heard, from people who have no interest in this matter, including the Sheriff, that jury does seem to have been rigged with the object of finding you guilty of that charge and seeing to it that you were hanged with the least possible delay. That, in itself, speaks to me more strongly than any of the vague tales that have been spread around New Orleans. That, and the fact that this Major Allenton obviously has faith in you.'

For a moment there was a deep silence, then Blaine said incredulously from the other side of the fire, 'You ain't meanin' to hire him as scout, are you, Roberts? If you do, you'll regret it when this wagon train goes the same way as that other. He'll get the information to those outlaws by some means, believe me.'

'I am the one who makes the decision,' said Roberts

tautly. He faced the other for a long moment and in the silent battle of wills, it was Blaine who backed down first. He shrugged as though washing his hands of the whole affair.

'Then the deaths of all the people with this train will be on your conscience, always assumin' that you get through alive,' he grunted. Viciously, he added as a final taunt, 'though maybe Dillman will see to it that they spare your life, for giving him this job.'

In a single blur of speed, so quickly that Blaine had no chance to move, Tracey was on his feet in a lithe movement, and around the side of the fire, one fist gripping the other's bunched up shirt tightly, pulling the man slightly off balance. He thrust his face close to the other's.

'You talk too much,' he said thinly. 'Now either put up or shut up.'

For a moment, Blaine stared at him as Tracey released his hold and stepped back a couple of paces, waiting. Then his pride turned yeasty in him. He licked his dry lips, running his tongue over them for a long moment, before saying: 'I figured you'd call me like that, mister. It's the usual way, isn't it, with your kind. Call a man when he's at a disadvantage and shoot him down in cold blood. Maybe you are faster than me with a gun, you seem to have had a lot more practice at it than I have. I'm not drawing on you. If you like to shoot a man down without that, go right ahead.'

'I might do that if you try to push me too far,' Tracey said warningly. He felt a little puzzled by the other's attitude in this matter. Just where had this man come from before he had linked up with this wagon train. There was a tiny germ of suspicion at the back of his mind but it refused to crystallize or come out into the open where he could grasp it and recognize it for what it was.

He grew aware that the other man was shaking his head slowly, almost positively. 'You won't do that,' he said tightly. 'Gunmen like you seem to have this code of letting the other man draw first before you shoot. Could be that it eases your conscience a little.' The sharp glitter died from

his face by degrees. He said finally, to Roberts. 'I'm tellin'
you, you'll be makin' a big mistake letting this man ride
with you.'

'I'll take that chance,' Roberts said slowly. He looked a
little distrubed but whether it was because of Blaine or
himself, Tracey could not tell.

That night, Tracey rode out of the wagon camp and into
New Orleans. Making a slow swing around the nearer
houses, he paused halfway along one of the streets to sit
his mount and search the shadows closely, gaze wandering
in a wide circle. Nothing moved there, yet he knew that
someone stood in those dark shadows and a few moments
later, he saw the brief stabbing red spark of a cigarette tip
at the side of one of the long, low-roofed stores. Stepping
down from his mount after casting a quick glance behind
him in the direction from which he had come, he angled
between two of the buildings, came up into the narrow
alley, close to where the short man stood, shoulders lounging against the wall, a man seemingly interested only in
smoking his cigarette and contemplating the night
around him.

Then the other's voice came to him from the shadows,
slow and easy: 'You fixed up yet, Dillman?'

'Yes, the train on the trail just outside town. They'll be
moving off day after tomorrow. Reckon you'd better get
word through to the Major.'

'Sure, I can do that.' The other gave a quick nod in the
darkness. The tip of his cigarette glowed a crimson brightness as he drew deeply on it. The faint glow of starlight
touched his face, highlighting the scar on his right cheek.
'You have any trouble this time?'

'Some,' Tracey admitted. 'There was one *hombre* there
tried to make trouble. He'd recognized me, evidently
didn't want me with 'em.'

'Well, we expected that,' went on the other softly. He
took a final long drag at his cigarette, then tossed the butt
into the dust and ground it in with his heel.

'This was somethin' different. I'm sure of that,' Tracey said. 'This *hombre* was spoilin' for a fight, but it was as if he wanted to do everythin' he could to stop me movin' out with them. I've got the oddest feelin' about that *hombre*, but I can't seem to put my finger on it right at the moment.'

'You reckon he's got some other reason for not wantin' you along?' queried the other, a faint ring of surprise in his tone.

'Could be. I figure I'd better keep an eye on him during the trail west. He claimed he wouldn't ride with the train if I went along, but Roberts – he's the wagon master – hired me on the spot, and I figure this man will come along too.'

'Well, it's no business of mine whether he does or not, I reckon,' said the other. He straightened up from his attitude against the wall, pushed his hat a little further back on his head with a thumb. 'I'd better make tracks back to the outpost with this news. But move easy once you're with the train. We don't want anythin' to go wrong this time and remember, you may not be so lucky the next time.'

'I'll bear that in mind,' Tracey said grimly. He stepped aside from the shed suddenly, head cocked a little to one side and gave the street at his back a careful study. He thought he had heard a sudden scuffle not far away, as though a man had moved incautiously in the darkness, heels slipping a little in the dust that lay like a blanket over everything here in this side street.

'What's wrong?' asked the other now, in a low, sharp tone, moving forward a little, one hand dropping towards the gun at his belt.

'I'm not sure. Thought I heard somebody movin' around close by. Don't see anybody there now. Must've been my imagination.'

'Could have been,' acknowledged the other after a brief pause. He turned his head slowly to take in all of the seeable view around them. 'You sure you weren't followed from the camp?'

'Sure of it,' Tracey was positive of that. 'But I reckon

there could've been some of the men from the train here in town this evening, maybe at one of the saloons and it could have been one of them who had spotted me here.'

'If it was, it might mean truble. Some of them suspect you already and if you were seen talkin' to me like this, they might start puttin' two and two together and comin' up with some other answers.'

'That's a risk we'll have to take,' Tracey said tightly. He had already thought of that possibility and he didn't like it. He nodded to the other. 'Just you get that information back to Major Allenton. I'll scout around and see if I can find anythin' and then head back for the wagon train. If there is any trouble there, I'll handle it.' He spoke with a quiet confidence. For a moment the other looked up at him, eyes searching his face, then he gave a swift, brief nod and slipped back into the dark, encircling shadows that closed them in.

Tracey waited until the man had gone, vanishing like a ghost into the darkness, then he padded softly forward, circling the nearest store, treading cat-like in the dust, making no sound whatever. He reached the point where he reckoned he had heard the slight sound, bent and peered hard at the ground in front of him. There were marks there all right, marks of a man's boots. He nodded to himself in the darkness, a sudden grimness in his mind. Had the man who had been standing here a few moments before, seen anything? Had he heard anything? And what was most important, had he recognized him?

If he had been seen and recognized, the news would be spread around the wagon train before morning and he would have a lot of awkward questions to answer. He knit his brows and tried to figure out who it might have been. Any of the other men in the train would scarcely have recognized him in the darkness and at that distance. Only Roberts, the wagon-master and Blaine knew him sufficiently well by now to have known him. Roberts, he felt sure, would have come forward, would not have skulked there in the shadows like an ordinary bushwhacker. But Blaine was a different proposition . . .

Cautiously, he edged forward along the side of the store, keeping one hand trailing along the smooth wood. He reached the end, held himself well in, then risked a quick look around the corner. The alley that stretched away at the back of the store was empty, deserted. Nothing moved as far as the eye could see. Then something moved swiftly across the alley and he started, clawing for his gun, before he heard the faint yowl of an alley cat. He thrust the gun back into its holster with a faintly muttered curse. He was getting far too jumpy. He would have to control himself a lot better than this, he told himself fiercely.

Carefully, he went forward, eyes scanning the dark shadows on either side of him. Finally, however, he was forced to admit that whoever had been there had managed to slip away without being seen. A moment later, as if in answer to that question in his mind, he heard the sudden start of a horse in the main street less than a hundred yards away. Moving quickly, he came out of the alley mouth, just in time to see the horse and rider spurring out of town, the man bent low over his mount's neck. It was impossible to tell who it was, but there had been something oddly familiar about the other that he had vaguely recognized. Troubled, he made his way back to where his own horse was tethered, loosened off the bridle, swung up into the saddle and rode out along the trail which led to the encampment. There were two fires blazing brightly in the middle of the wagons, and the red light of the leaping flames threw huge, wavering shadows over the Conestogas.

There were several men seated around the fire when Tracey rode up. He slid from the saddle well outside the firelight, tethered his horse to the hitching rope, then went along the line of horses there, checking each one. It did not take him long to find the one which had recently been ridden hard. It was sweat-lathered, had not been rubbed down by its owner, but one glance was enough for him to realize that it was, as he had suspected, Blaine's mount. So it was the big, loud-mouthed man who had seen him back there in New Orleans. Now, if the other needed it, he had something to use against him. He went forward slowly, setting his feet carefully over the tongue of one of the wagons. He could just make out the other standing just inside the circle of firelight, whittling away at a piece of wood with the razor-sharp edge of his Bowie knife. The man looked up as he strode towards the fire, but beyond the look of hatred that burned at the back of the deep-set eyes, he said nothing, then glanced down again, went back to his whittling. But there had been that faint, secret smile on his thick lips and Tracey could guess at the reason for it.

He seated himself at the fire. A few yards away, around the other fire, one of the men was singing something softly to himself, strumming an ancient guitar. It was an old song from before the war, a song that told of a land where the sun was always warm, where the people were free and there was no poverty, where a woman's arms were warm and her lips soft. Tracey felt a strange glow come to him as he listened to the words. Maybe that was how all of these people thought of California, a place where they could shed all of their worries and live in peace. How many would find it to be a country like that, even if they managed to get there, he did not know.

There was talk at the fire of what lay ahead of them when they pulled out. Listening, Tracey guessed that more than half of them had little idea of the dangers and privations they would have to meet when they set out. Soon, he thought, after they had been on the trail for a little while, they would become hardened, they would realize there were many difficulties they would have to face, many trials and tribulations they would have to undergo before they got to the Promised Land of California.

They made good time that first day on the trail. The horses were fresh and the wagons were well sprung and not too heavily loaded. Tracey rode scout, drifting ahead, keeping his eyes open, knowing a little of what to look for this time. And always, as he rode, he was aware of the other rider out on the far side of the trail, the big figure of Blaine, riding with a hard face, thinking his own thoughts which were kept hidden behind the perpetual scowl that creased his features.

Sooner or later, Tracey knew, the other was going to try something and he would have to be ready when the showdown came. But it would not be yet. Blaine was no fool and although he probably considered himself something of a gunman, he did not intend to risk his life finding out just how good Tracey was with a gun. He would wait his time until he could take the other unawares, and most likely while they were out of sight of the train. Blaine did not want any of the others to be witnesses if it came to the point where he shot Tracey in the back. There would be some kind of law and order in California if they got there and he would not be able to escape punishment if he tried anything like that and his actions were discovered.

That night, they made camp in low scrub below a high ridge that stretched for the best part of a mile along the side of the trail. They were now well to the south of the trail Tracey had taken to the outpost, would eventually pass maybe forty or fifty miles to the south of the camp. He wondered if that man who had met him in New Orleans had managed to get through all right with the news. A lot was clearly going to depend on that, he reflected tightly.

They bedded the cattle they had brought with them, tied off to the ends of the wagons while they were on the trail, then retired themselves early. There was to be a quick start in the morning, before the sun got too strong. Only the two men left on watch remained awake, seated by the fire, occasionally stirring themselves to check the horses and the terrain around the camp. Lying in his blankets, Tracey watched them for a long moment, then reached out and acting on impulse, pulled the Winchester closer to him until it was lying under him with one arm thrown out over it.

There was silence in the camp except for the snap and crackle of the flames as they ate hungrily at the dry wood on the fires. One of the men who had been out to check the horses came back with an armful of wood and tossed it on to the nearer fire. For a moment it damped down the flames, then they caught and sparks lifted twenty, thirty feet into the still night air, drifting up in spirals as the draught from the fire below caught them, whirling them away. The darkness over the camp seemed sharpened by the myriad pinpoints of light that were the stars.

The next day they continued to head west, and the next. Day followed day in the same, endless rhythm. The heat burned them, sapped their strength, took the moisture from their bodies and left them weak and dehydrated. The horses were also affected by it, and progress slowed. Still, they had not reached the Badlands. Only Tracey knew what to expect once they ran into the Alkali Flats. He spoke to Roberts about it on the day before they were due to hit them.

'I've been this trail before. Pretty soon we'll have to cross the Flats and it won't be easy or pleasant. Think you ought to warn the others what they're heading into?'

'How long do you say it ought to take us?' demanded the other, his sharp-eyed gaze quartering the horizon ahead of them, as though straining to push his sight clear across the skyline to the Flats which lay there somewhere in the sun-hazed, heat-shivering distance.

'Three days, I figure, if we can made good time. There's a river before we hit them where we'll have to fill every cask and barrel we can with water to last us across. The horses and cattle will have to go without or get short rations. But we should make it.'

'Is there no way around these Flats?'

Tracey gave a nod. 'Sure there is, but it will take us far to the north and add several days to our journey.'

'It might be worthwhile considerin' that, instead of risking the journey over the Flats.'

Tracey gave a dubious nod. 'That's possible, but we

have only so much food and until we can shoot some game for ourselves, we'll have to go on short rations. Better to head over the alkali, I reckon.'

The other pondered that for a long moment, sitting easily on the tongue of the wagon, then he gave a brief shrug. 'Very well,' he said with a faint sigh, 'that's the way we go. Scout ahead and check on the river. If it's dry, as it may be out here, we may have to revise our plans and head north whether we like it or not.'

Tracey nodded, touched spurs to his horse, rode away from the slow-moving wagon train. In front of him, the ground became more open. The trail was still a wide stretch of beaten dust, unsullied as yet, but soon to be kicked up by the hooves of the horses and cattle, the grinding wheels of the wagons. Soon, the wagon train was out of sight, lost in the distance behind him. He gave his horse its head. Brown earth soon gave way to the red, muddy clay which gave an indication that he was approaching the river. A quick glance told him that the clay was moist underfoot, a good sign. Scrub oak and hackberry dotted the ground around him and within two hours he came on the rolling grasslands which bordered the river on this side of the Flats. There would be grazing here for the horses and cattle before they began that terrible drive over the Flats. It was as if Nature were willing to temper some of the wilderness with a little kindness.

He rode on, over the rolling plains until he sighted the river and off in the distance, there was the blinding white of the Flats, stretching away to the far horizon, further than the eye could see, a brilliant, glaring white that hurt the eyes to look at it for long and sent a little apprehensive shiver through him as he remembered his last ride across them. In spite of himself, of the tight grip he had on his mind and his emotions, the fear was there, deep within him, bubbling a little to the surface.

The river was a foot below its full flood height, moving with a slow, ponderous current between its banks, bearing down a few branches from higher in the hills where it had its origin. They ought to have little difficulty crossing it, he reckoned. The big Conestoga wagons were never easy to handle when it came to crossing a river as wide as this, and he could not tell how deep it might be in the middle where the current was strongest. But at least the river was not in flood. He scouted along the bank for a little way, then wheeled his mount and rode back, giving the news to Roberts.

'Then you figure we can get the wagons across?'

'Sure. It was worse the last time and they managed it all right. Maybe get a couple of riatas tied off the backs to keep 'em swinging straight when the current hits 'em, but that's all.'

'And there's grass for the horses and cattle?'

'Plenty. Maybe we ought to rest up a couple of days there, give 'em the best chance we can of getting across those Flats alive and as quickly as possible.'

Blaine, seated on his horse nearby, gave a sneering laugh. 'What's the matter, cowboy?' he called harshly. 'Scared of gettin' your feet wet?'

Tracey stared across at him, his glance cold. Carefully, he said: 'I reckon you ain't never ridden this trail before, Blaine, otherwise you'd know what a devil's cauldron that country is on the other side of the river. There are plenty of bones yonder to testify to men who thought they knew everythin' there was to know about the Flats and found to their cost that they were wrong.'

The sneer remained on the other's face. He swung on Roberts. 'If we're goin' to stick around for a couple of days every time we come up against somethin' like this, Roberts, I figure we're never goin' to make it to California. We have to make good time at the beginning, otherwise we'll be bogged down by the snows on the mountains further west. This ain't no time to listen to cowards, tellin' us to halt up and rest.'

Tracey stared into Blaine's eyes, a hard light in his irises, but the anger cooled quickly in Tracey. He knew the other was doing his best to rile him, and thrust the thought away.

The anger hadn't vanished, only gone chilly, like a tight hand of ice around his heart. For a long moment, his gaze locked with the other's, then Blaine turned away with a muttered snort intended to be one of derision and rode off, kicking up a cloud of dust behind him.

Roberts stared after him for a long moment with a frown of worried concentration on his broad features. He said softly after a moment: 'There's something about that man I'm not certain of, Dillman. What it is I don't know, but I have a feeling he'll be a bad man to tangle with.' He let his gaze drop to Tracey, a tightness at the edges of his mouth.

The meaning behind his words was quite clear. Tracey said: 'So long as he doesn't start any real trouble with me, I won't be the one to begin anything, Mr Roberts. But if he tries to push me too far, I won't answer for the consequences.'

'I know. That's what troubles me. I've heard a little about you and I know you're faster with a gun than he is, but he's cunning like a coyote and he'll shoot you in the back without batting an eyelid.'

'I'll keep an eye on him,' Tracey promised. He wheeled his mount, rode off the trail to the side of the wagon train as the Conestogas rumbled forward, greased axles grinding in the wood and metal. The women peered out from the canvas, trying to get a breath of fresh air, but here there was little to be had. The ground threw back the tremendous heat of the sun, reflecting it up into their eyes and faces and the interiors of the wagons were like ovens, with not a breath of air stirring.

They cut into the wide grasslands that afternoon, late, with the sun dipping horizonwards, throwing shadows about them. Now the country lifted from its rolling flatness and gave way to undulating hills, interspersed with dunes of sand and then clay as they neared the river's bank. Here and there, a cluster of tall pines rose up from the ground, gaunt sentinels guarding the way to the low hills. They pulled up a steep rise, the animals straining in the traces, men getting down to put their shoulders to the rear wheels, heaving with all of their strength as the sweat poured from their faces and dripped from their chins on to the ground below them. Then they had topped the rise and in front of them, pleasant and bringing a refreshing colour to tired, gritty eyes, lay the long, wide grasslands which grew on the eastern bank of the great river. Out of the corner of his eye, Tracey saw the change that come over the people in the wagons. He heard a loud whoop from somewhere behind him, saw a man pointing a finger to where it was just possible to make out the water. The animals smelled it, nostrils dragging in the scent of the water even above the nearer, more dominating scent of the lush grass. They pulled more easily now, lengthening their stride, the wagons rumbling forward through the grass.

But there were three men who looked beyond the grass and the river. Tracey sat atop a tall rise, sitting easily in the saddle, shading his eyes against the red glare of the sun, eyeing the harsh whiteness that could be seen in the distance, the alkali desert which they would have to cross within the next few days.

On the rolling tongue of the lead wagon, Roberts stretched himself up to his full height, still holding the reins tightly in his broad-fingered hands, eyes staring off into the distance, where the heat shimmer touched the whiteness and he felt a growing hardness in his stomach like a stone settling there. The muscles of his chest tightened just a shade as he recalled what he had heard of this hell land.

Further off to the left, Blaine rode his mount cruelly, spurring it forward. He was perhaps three quarters of a mile from the train now, still in sight of them, and he knew that he could not act suspiciously for fear of being spotted. There was a tall, steep-sided butte standing up from the plain over to his left and he spurred towards it, fighting the animal as it tried to slow its mad pace, not giving it any rest until they had clambered stiff-legged up the winding, rocky trail and he was almost on top of the rise, where he could look out over the stretching terrain and see for many miles in every direction. He glimpsed the wagon train far off to his right and beyond it, a tiny speck which he guessed was Tracey Dillman, stopped near one of the ledges.

Then he turned his attention to the ground directly ahead of him, looking beyond the river, beyond the Flats which stretched away in a blaze of eye-searing white, towards the far hills that lifted on the skyline to the west. There was a small spy-glass in his saddle bag and he pulled it out, squinting along it at the hills, moving it slowly from right to left. He could see nothing and yet he felt certain there should have been a sign of some kind. By now, either Laredo or Carrico ought to have had word that the train was approaching.

He sucked in his lips, lowered the glass for a moment, contemplated his position. Soon, he would have to slip away from the train to join up with the others in the hills. Laredo and Carrico would be glad to hear of that new type of rifle Dillman was carrying in his saddle scabbard. He had not been able to get close enough to it to examine it as thoroughly as he would have liked, but from what he had seen of it, it looked like a new type of repeating rifle and Carrico and the others could run into trouble if they came in, not expecting something like this.

He rubbed his chin absently for a moment, then lifted the glass again, focused it and stared through it at the tall mountains. For a moment, the scene was as before. Then he paused, muttered an exclamation of satisfaction under his breath as he held himself rigid in the saddle. He exhaled slowly. There was a thin column of smoke lifting from close to one of the peaks. It was the signal he had been hoping for. Closing the glass, he thrust it back into his saddle-bag, wheeled his mount and headed back to the train.

When men had long distances to cover, especially across

such a terrible wilderness as the Flats, the best way, perhaps the only way, was to go slowly. Too much speed resulted in broken axles, in wagons half-buried in the shifting alkali. They had crossed the river without incident and were now more than halfway over the Flats. The dust lay all about them, stinging and choking, even though they rode with neckerchiefs across the lower half of their faces and the women and children were all inside the wagons, with the canvas battened down on all sides. It did not succeed in keeping all of the dust out, for it managed to filter everywhere, even through cracks which were not visible to the naked eye. But the terrible heat was better than the agonies which the men and animals were forced to suffer in that long drive over the Flats. Men had called these the Badlands, and it was an apt name. Nothing could grow here. In this dry, caustic dust it was impossible to imagine anything that could survive in this wilderness.

Always, it would be a scar on the face of the earth, untamed, shunned by men who could find some way around it; and when that was not possible and it had to be crossed, they endured the agonies of the damned as they moved forward, half blinded by the tremendous glare, bodies racked and tortured by the blistering heat, flesh rubbed raw by the dust and grit, eyeballs burned and sore.

Nothing relieved the piled-up intensity of the heat head. Long as he had followed the trails throughout the whole of the South, this land was punishment to Tracey. The edges of the bridle held the heat, burning to the touch and the metal pieces threw vicious, stabbing flashes of light into his eyes. He lifted his neckpiece higher over his nose, screwing up his eyes against the dust cloud which clung to the air.

It was just possible to make out the edge of the Flats in the far distance and he figured that with luck, they ought to cross them by the next day. With the setting of the sun, the brief coolness came and then the bitter chill of the desert night. There was such a short time when the temperature was pleasant, he thought dully, as he climbed down from his mount as they made camp. Seated on the edge of the small fire which had been built with the pieces of dry wood they carried with them for such a contingency, he kept his eyes on Blaine as the big fellow shuffled forward after riding in from scouting to the south of the train. He seated himself cross-legged near the fire, held out his hands towards the blaze. He seemed unduly preoccupied, Tracey thought, glancing unobtrusively in the other's direction, as if he had something important on his mind. More and more, Tracey was growing suspicious of the other, feeling certain that Blaine was either running from something and had joined the wagon train to get the chance of slipping out of the state; or he was heading into something. If the law was on his heels, then there was little to fear from him, so long as he considered he was safe. But if he was with the train to keep an eye on things, until he might ride out and warn the outlaws who were probably lying in wait for them, then there was great danger for everyone with the train.

That night, he lay awake in his blankets, feeling the bitter cold seep into his bones in spite of the warmth of the fire. But it helped to keep him from falling asleep and on this particular night he was anxious not to succumb to the weariness in his body. After these days on the trail, every man became weary, slept like logs during the night, did not wish to waken in the morning, before dawn when they had to be up and ready, eating a quick, hurried meal before moving out again.

He kept his eyes on the hump of shadow that was Blaine, sleeping in his blankets on the far side of the fire. He did not anticipate that the other would make his move until they were over the river at the western edge of the Flats. Then would be the time when he would slip away, if he intended to. There was little doubt in Tracey's mind now as to the real reason why Blaine was with them on this train, nor why he had been so keen to stop Tracey from joining it back in New Orleans. Possibly he recognized that Tracey would represent the biggest danger to himself and the outlaws; a man who had seen everyone killed around him on that other train that had tried to get through the outlaw infested hills in the west. And there was also that link-up between him and the Major. No doubt Blaine had been wondering and worrying about that too on the way.

As he lay there, turning these thoughts over in his mind, he began to find that a lot of little things which had been puzzling him during the past week or so, were now beginning to fit into place and make some kind of sense. Indian Pete had been killed, shot in the back somewhere along the trail, to prevent him from telling what he knew. The outlaws had to have someone else they could trust in New Orleans to pass on the vital information and there seemed little doubt that Blaine was their man.

He remained awake throughout the night, but Blaine made no move during the long, cold hours, sleeping innocently in his blankets, rising when the dawn broke with a steely grey in the east, covering the desert with an eerie flush of white.

By the time the sun came up, they were moving out on their last lap over the Flats. The wagons rolled through the ankle-deep dust and occasionally became bogged down and had to be hauled free of the alkali that sifted over the axles in places. It was hard, back-breaking work. Even under more congenial conditions, it would have been difficult, but as it was, with the dust swirling about them, getting down into their lungs with every breath they took, it was sheer agony to keep on the move. Yet somehow, they forced their flagging muscles to obey their wills and shortly before five o'clock that evening, the ground began to rise and they emerged from the flat bowl of the desert and began to head in the direction of the river. The cattle, tied off to the backs of the wagons, lifted their great heads, nostrils flared as they drew in the smell of distant water, and then they began to bawl loudly, tugging at the ropes that held them, pawing at the dry ground underfoot, anxious to be away.

The sun dropped behind the hills. The world gave up its redness and its heat and became blue and cool, with the smell of the hills in the air, moist and refreshing after the bitter burnt-out smell of the desert. Coolness flowed around them taking away the sting of the desert from their bodes. The canvas covers were thrown back to let the air blow through the wagons. The horses increased their gait and before nightfall, they were at the river. They formed up the wagons in the inevitable circle, built their fires and posted guards. From this point on, they could expect trouble, Tracey told them.

They listened seriously and only Blaine dissented from this view. Getting to his feet, the other said loudly and harshly, 'All the time we've been on the trail we've listened to him tellin' us about how dangerous it's goin' to be. We were told that it would be difficult crossin' the Flats. Well we're here ain't we, without any trouble. Now he tells us that we can except to be jumped by outlaws anywhere along the trail. If you ask me, he's got outlaws on the brain. Maybe if he was to do his job right, and scout ahead, he might know for sure if any of these outlaws are around.'

'Seems to me that you're doin' a heap of talking,' said Tracey quietly. He remained seated by the fire, staring up at the other, his tone flat and without emotion.

Blaine swore, then gave an ugly laugh. 'I'm willin' to ride out tonight and scout across that river yonder,' he said. There was an edge to his tone that Tracey had not heard before and he began to wonder at it.

He got up. He was aware that Roberts and several of the other men had their eyes on him, wondering what he was going to do. Maybe they had heard that he was innocent of that charge which had been brought against him in New Orleans, but after all, there had been some irregularities there, with the Major bursting in on the trial after the jury had found him guilty, and it was just possible that the seed of doubt was still in their minds and they were remembering what Blaine had said before they had pulled out.

'You know, it could be you've got a special reason for wantin' to ride out scoutin' tonight, Blaine,' he said softly.

'Just what are you meanin' by that?' demanded the other, blustering a little.

'Just this. I've been watchin' you ever since we pulled across the Flats. You always seem anxious to ride off alone, staying away from the train as much as possible, even when there was no need for scouting because we were in the middle of that desert and they stretch for miles in every direction. I'm figurin' that you've got some friends up ahead, waitin' for you to show up, waiting for you to give them some information on this train, the trail we'll be takin', how many men we have and the kind of guns.'

Blaine's rage boiled over at that. For a moment, his thick lips worked, but no sound came out. Then he jerked out: 'Why, you lyin' killer. Nobody is goin' to accuse me of that and get away with it.'

A tight, thin-lipped smile crossed Tracey's lips. He moved a little distance away from the fire, bringing himself in line with the other, his legs braced a little, arms swinging by his sides. He said in thin tones, glacial with menace. 'Just what are you figurin' on doin' about it, Blaine?'

'Stop that, both of you,' said Roberts harshly. He stepped up between the two men. 'I'll have no shooting here. You've both said enough.'

'He said too much,' retorted Blaine thickly. His neck seemed to be more swollen than usual, the veins standing out like cords under the skin. 'Who does he think he is, speaking to me like that? Just because that Major got him off from the hanging he deserved, after the jury had found him guilty, he reckons that it makes him innocent. The Major ain't around here any more to wet-nurse him.'

'Forget it,' snapped Roberts. 'Now I don't want to hear any more of this between you two men while you're with this wagon train. Understand?'

Blaine sneered, ignoring Roberts to turn and glower at

Tracey. Then he whirled on his heel and stalked off into the darkness that lay beyond the glow of the fire. Tracey forced himself to relax. His fingers straightened and he sat down again by the fire. He did not doubt that he had hit the truth when he had accused him of wanting to ride out to meet the outlaw band in the hills. He would have to make his move that night.

The half-moon was just setting behind the western bluffs. Soon it was gone and darkness settled over the land, lying on the grassland which bordered the river. Tracey lay in his blankets, listening intently to the night sounds all about him. In the desert, there had been few sounds to disturb the stillness, but here there seemed to be something moving in every direction. The grass rustled in the breeze that blew from the hills and there was the faint sound of the river lapping against its banks. A horse snickered nearby and it was answered a few moments later by one of the steers tethered off to one side of the camp. Tracey rolled over and eased himself up on one elbow, peering into the blackness around him. At first, he could hear and see nothing out of the ordinary. Then his eyes caught the sudden movement off to one side, well beyond the glow of the dying fire. Narrowing his eyes, he paused, then stiffened as he saw the dark shape glide up from the ground and edge away from the camp, pausing only to clamber silently over the bent tongue of one of the wagons. He did not need to get any closer to the man to know who it was.

He had expected Blaine to try to slip away sometime during the night. Now it was obvious he was not going to be disappointed. Gently, he eased himself out of the blanket, crawled for a couple of yards on his hands and knees, then moved upright into the blackness around the camp, gripping the Winchester in his right hand.

By the time he had reached the point where the horses were tethered, he had lost Blaine. The other had taken his mount and had walked him off into the distance before mounting up. A few seconds later, he picked out the sound of hoofbeats in the distance, moving away. Swiftly, he loosened his own mount, swung up into the saddle and let the horse have its head, cutting after the other. Whatever happened, he had to stop Blaine before he reached the rest of the outlaws who were undeniably waiting for him somewhere in the distance.

He spurred his mount forward. By now, his eyes had grown used to the darkness and a few moments later, topping a low rise that overlooked the river at this point he caught a glimpse of the other, riding away into the night, cutting over the flat terrain towards the river. Blaine did not once look behind him, nor slow the pace of his mount. Clearly, he thought he had managed to slip away from the camp without being seen and was not expecting any pursuit.

Grimly, Tracey guided his horse forward, putting it down the slope, the soft ground muffling the sound of its hooves. He was gaining slowly on the other, but he knew he dared not go too close for fear of being spotted if the other should turn in his saddle and glance over his shoulder and he could not risk a shot with the rifle at that distance, warning the other of his presence. The moon went down and there was only the faint starlight to show him the running figure of the other rider.

He guessed that the other would slow when he reached the river's bank, and casting his gaze ahead, pushing his sight through the dimness, Tracey managed to make out the shallows directly ahead of him and the faint scar of a trail which wound across the prairie on the far side of the river, cutting eventually across the track that Blaine was evidently taking.

Wheeling his mount's head, he put it on the downgrade, straight for the river, hit the water in a flying leap that put him well into the shallows. In the middle of the river, the horse breasted the current, swimming strongly. A few moments later, Tracey slid from its back, clinging to the reins and went into the water, being dragged forward by the horse.

Once it began stepping up into the higher ground on the far side, he climbed back into the saddle, and rode off into the darkness, cutting across to the other trail. He saw no sight of Blaine now, could not make out the drumming of the other's horse, but he felt no real concern. The outlaws Blaine was clearly going to meet would be waiting some miles away, they would not risk being so close to where the train had camped. A mile further on, he caught the faint break of hoofbeats on the hard ground, then Blaine was a vague motion in front of him and he knew that his hunch had paid off.

SEVEN

Wild Men Waiting

Shifting his position was no longer an easy matter for Tracey. The other would spot him within minutes now, could not fail to do so as he was coming towards him from the side. But in spite of this, Tracey went forward with a bold speed on the angle which eventually put him just a little ahead of the other and to the side of Blaine's trail. All he had to do now was wait off the trail for the other to appear. Gently, he slid the Winchester from its scabbard, relishing the feel of the gun. If a traitor and killer like Blaine had to die then he felt it was only just that he should die by this gun and no other, he thought tensely.

A moment later, Blaine came around the bend in the trail perhaps twenty feet away. He saw Tracey's mount almost at once and reined hard, freezing where he stood. It was obvious that he did not, as yet, recognize the man who sat there, waiting for him. Then his voice came questioningly from the darkness.

'That you, Laredo? It's Blaine.'

Tracey smiled grimly. The other's words told him everything he wanted to know. Very softly, he said: 'You just made your last mistake, Blaine.'

There was an instant stiffening of the other's body from knees to shoulders. He said hoarsely: 'Dillman – you!'

'That's right. The last man you expected to find. You

tried to get me framed with those settlers in New Orleans as a man who would betray them to the outlaws. But you're the man who's betraying 'em. I had you figured this way for a little while, but you had to lead me here before I could be sure.'

'Damn you, Dillman. Reckon you'd better put up that rifle, before you get yourself shot in the back. You don't reckon I'd come ridin' out here alone, do you?' There was a slight break in the other's voice.

Tracey shook his head very slowly. He knew that the outlaws were not within a mile or more of this place and they would not come riding up yet to see what was happening.

'Save your breath,' he said thinly. 'You know better than to try that trick. Your outlaw friends are a few miles away yet and they won't help you.'

'Listen,' said the other hurriedly, recognizing that Tracey had the drop on him. He spoke with an unnecessary loudness, speaking hurriedly so that the words seemed to tumble over themselves in a torrent. 'There's a lot in this. More money than you've ever dreamed of and you could have your share. What do you care about those folk on the wagon train? They're the same kind as those men in New Orleans who rigged a jury so as to be sure of hanging you. They don't care whether you're dead or alive.'

'Blaine,' said Tracey, his voice going soft and quiet amid the rocks so that it carried no further than the man in front of him. 'Blaine, I knew a long while ago that sooner or later we'd meet up like this, just the two of us, and that only one of us would ride away from the meetin'.'

The other's lips thinned, drew back from his teeth. He pulled himself up taut and straight in the saddle, not taking his eyes from Tracey's rifle. 'You aimin' to shoot me down in cold blood without a chance?'

'I ought to. Gettin' an even break is only for men, not four-flushers like you.'

The other shrugged. He let his hands move slow as

though to rest them on the pommel of his saddle. Then, with a shocking abruptness, he clawed for the guns in his holsters. They were half clear of leather when Tracey pulled the trigger. The rifle blasted loud and strong in the saddle, then he arched back over the rim of his saddle, remained like that for a long moment before he somehow managed to drag himself upright again, a look of shocked disbelief on his face. Then a gush of red came from his open mouth and spilled down his chin as he toppled from the saddle, pitching into the dust. His horse reared and careened against the rocks, then ran on, dragging the dead body of the outlaw behind it for a little way before his foot was shaken loose from the reins and he lay among the rocks, the horse continuing in its flight into the rocky ravines.

Tracey thrust the rifle back into its scabbard, sat for a moment staring down at the inert body of Blaine, then turned and headed back to the river. The sound of that shot would have carried for a great distance in the night stillness and if those outlaws that Blaine had been riding to meet were anywhere in the vicinity, they must surely have heard it and known that something had gone wrong.

At the camp, he found three of the men still awake, the two guards and Roberts, the wagon master. The other came pushing forward as Tracey rode in, climbed down from the saddle and tied his mount to the rope.

'All right, Dillman,' said the other harshly. 'What happened? One of the men said he saw you ride off some time ago. He yelled, but you didn't come back.' His tone hardened just a shade and the lines around the corners of his mouth deepened as he laid his gaze on the other.

'Blaine is dead,' Tracey said simply. 'I spotted him slipping out of camp and decided to follow him. I've had my suspicions about that man ever since he tried to sway you against me before we left New Orleans. He seemed too intent on discrediting me. Then, I caught a glimpse of him while we were crossing the Flats, he was a mile or so away, but it was pretty clear he was using some kind of spy-glass to watch the hills yonder, evidently lookin' for a signal from his friends.'

'I see.' The other stood waiting for him to go on, stony-patient. 'Did he meet up with the outlaws?'

'No, I caught up with him before he could do that. But when he saw me he asked if I was Laredo. I knew then that I'd got him dead to rights. He went for his guns and I shot him. His body is back there in the trail someplace, but you won't find it if you was to ride out now. That shot will have been heard and the outlaws will have dragged him away.'

'Then you figure it's safe for us to go on?' The other drew his brows together, regarded Tracey sharply.

'We've got no other choice,' he said tightly. He seemed to remember having said that sometime before and he had led the wagon train into disaster. Would there be any difference this time, or would the same thing happen, the outlaws forewarned about them, ready in even bigger numbers than before, determined not to let a single one of them escape this time. Then he remembered the word he had passed on to Major Allenton's man, knew that if the other had got through to the outpost, they might be able to sway the battle in their favour, if only he and the men on the train could hold off the outlaws long enough for the soldiers to get down from the north, for there had been no chance to slip any of Allenton's men in with the train, not with Blaine evidently ready to get any word at all to the outlaws.

He had spotted nothing of the Major's men, if they were there at all. At times on the trail, he had stared off to the north, eyes searching for a dust cloud lifted by horses, any sign at all that would tell him the wagon train was not completely alone in this wilderness, but there had been nothing. Now he was not even sure that the man from New Orleans had managed to get through. Indian Pete had probably been running away and he would have known those trails far better than that soldier, and he had been shot in the back, without a chance to defend himself. If Blaine had managed to get word to somebody before riding back to camp that night he had seen Tracey talking in the shadows near the storehouses, it was possible that the Major had not received word about the wagon train, and had done nothing. If that was the case, then they were riding to their deaths; not only himself, but every man, woman and child in the wagons. The thought sent a little shiver coursing along his back and it was only with a tremendous effort of will that he managed to push the idea out of his brain and concentrate on what Roberts was saying.

'If you figure we're safe, then we'll cross the river in the morning and head across country. It was in that narrow pass we saw just before dark that you were ambushed the last time wasn't it?'

'That's right,' nodded Tracey grimly. 'But this time it's goin' to be different, I promise you.'

Roberts still looked dubious. 'I certainly hope so,' he said harshly. 'I've got the lives of everyone on this train to think of and we can't afford to take any risks as far as they are concerned. Besides, if you're right in your suppositions about Blaine, then he may already have warned those friends of his up in the hills.'

'He may have. But there's only the one place where they can hit us and if you can let me have a handful of men, I reckon we can give these critters a surprise.'

'You've got a plan?' said the other.

'Sort of. There are one or two things I can't tell you yet, but if everything has gone well, I reckon we've got these polecats licked.'

'Well . . .' The other hesitated, then reached a sudden decision. 'All right, I'll do what you say, but by God if anything goes wrong and—'

Tracey gave a grim smile. He was not quite as sure of himself as he tried to appear but he tried to look confident. 'Be ready to move out at sun-up,' he said. 'The river's well down now and there won't be much trouble puttin' the wagons over. Then head straight for those bluffs yonder.'

'You aimin' to use us as bait?' demanded one of the guards harshly. 'I'll be damned if I'll agree to that. Now listen to me, Roberts, we hired you as wagon master to take us through to California, not to listen and fall in with any wild ideas that somebody like this drifter might put up. We've got our families in those wagons and our responsibility is towards them, not tryin' to trap a bunch of outlaws who probably outnumber us by ten to one. All professional killers into the bargain.'

'Like I said a minute ago,' put in Tracey. 'You've got no choice. You've come this far, but you can take my word for it those outlaws are lyin' across your trail, they've known every move you've made since we pulled out of New Orleans. Even if you tried to turn back now, they'd pick you off before you crossed the Flats. This is our only chance and like I said, we've got somethin' else up our sleeve though I can't talk about it yet, just in case Blaine wasn't the only spy among us. But you've got to trust me now, whatever happens.'

The man muttered something under his breath. 'Well, Jeb,' said Roberts. 'Do you agree, or don't you? Speak your peace.'

For a moment the other hesitated, his gaze boring into Tracey's. Then he shrugged. 'All right, but believe me, if you've led us into a trap, Dillman, you won't live to get anythin' out of it. I'll shoot you down before they get me, I promise you.'

'I figure I'll make it easy for you,' Tracey told the other soberly. 'I'd like you to be one of the men to ride out with me before first light.' If the other felt any surprise at the request, he did not show it, merely gave a surly nod of his head, gripping his rifle more tightly in his hands.

An hour before first light, Tracey was up, poking the dying embers of fire, bringing more light to it with a few of the dry faggots laid beside it. Then there was a movement among the wagons, shadowed in the faint light, and the other men who were to join him came out into the open, grim-faced men who had an inkling of what might lie ahead of them, carrying their weapons. They squatted by the fresh fire and soon there was the smell of food, as they ate an early breakfast then moved off to where their horses stood ready.

Anxious to be moving out, Tracey swung himself up into the saddle, waited impatiently for the others to come. He checked his Winchester, the two Colts in their holsters. The men were finally ready and lifting his right hand in salute to Roberts who stood beside one of the wagons, he led the men out of the camp, out to the river a half mile away. They forded it swiftly, scarcely slowing their mounts, climbed up the far bank, water pooling from the bellies of their horses, then they swung out to the north, moving into the rough, open country that lay beyond the bluffs. If Tracey had figured this right, then the outlaws would have camped overnight in the bluffs, just in case the wagon train moved off early, having been warned to a certain extent by what had happened to those other wagon trains that had been ambushed along the trail. If he and the men with him could move around without being seen, before the dawn brightened, they stood a good chance of getting into position above and behind the outlaws where they could cut in on them the minute they fired down on the wagon train. All of the men staying back with the wagons, knew what was expected of them. There were several in each wagon, armed with rifles and Colts, ready to meet the fire of the outlaws.

They rode hard, knowing they had some distance to cover before dawn and if they were still in the open country when the daylight came, they would be surely seen. But when the brightening new warmth of a fresh dawn spread over the country, rolling down from the hills to the west, they were well into the foothills of the bluffs, among the scrub oak and brush that grew in a wild profusion there, affording them plenty of cover on these gentler slopes.

They left their mounts out of sight where a small spring bubbled down the side of the slope and Tracey motioned upward to the narrow track that spiralled up to the high peaks of the bluffs. The men nodded in agreement, followed him in single file, gripping their rifles tightly, careful not to let them strike against the rocks on either side.

Minutes passed and lengthened into an hour. The sun lifted in the east and blazed down on them, the heat increasing with every passing minute. Tracey began to wish that the burning sun was not blasting on them so much. He could feel the sweat beginning to trickle down the small of his back and from under the sweatband of his hat. He sought for something to close his mind on during that terribly agonizing ascent, and found it by remembering Gideon Carter and the others who had been so foully murdered down there in the bluffs less than a mile away from them now. The thought of those killers already lying in wait among the rocks ahead of them, somewhere just over the high peaks of the bluffs, gave him the additional strength he needed to drive the weariness and lethargy away from his body.

The trail was steeper now, loose stones rolled and bounced from under their feet as they slipped on the treacherous ground. The top of the trail, where it wound up ahead of them, seemed as far away as ever and he began to despair of ever reaching it. 'The men too were breathing heavily, sweat streaming down their faces, but he drove them on like a madman, not giving them any respite, driving himself on to the very limit of his endurance. He knew that they would need of lot of their strength when it came to the showdown, but they had to reach the top before that wagon train came rolling into the canyon or it would be the finish for everyone in those wagons. He kept warning the others in a tight voice of what would happen to their wives and families if they did not obey him and somehow they did follow him, they found the strength and the endurance to struggle those last three hundred yards until suddenly they were climbing no longer, the peaks they had seen from below were now on a level with them.

The breath sobbing in his lungs, Tracey threw himself down on the narrow plateau at the top of the bluffs, motioned the rest of the men down beside him. They lay like dead men for several minutes, sucking air greedily into their lungs as though unable to extract sufficient oxygen from it for their bodily needs. Gradually, the life came back into their punished limbs and they were able to move again as Tracey motioned them slowly forward. Now there was danger, the chance of being seen by one of the look outs that the outlaws might have posted among the heights to watch for the approach of the wagon train. He tried to recall everything that had happened the last time he had been in these bluffs. He had ridden one of these higher trails with Denton and they had seen nothing. Yet there must have been someone up there, keeping an eye on the trail from the river, unless they had deliberately kept themselves out of sight in the scrub that lined the twisting trails, not meaning to give themselves away even though he and Denton had probably ridden so close to them that it would have been the easiest thing in the world to have dropped them both in the saddles. But that would have meant that the men on the train would have been warned that there was something wrong when they did not return.

'See anythin'?' grunted one of the men hoarsely. Tracey shook his head as he peered down the far slope, eyes searching for any sign of the outlaws. He could see nothing. Lifting his head a little, he searched the opposite slopes, beyond the narrow trail that meandered between the tall, rearing bluffs. Nothing there either, he thought, worried – and then he paused, pulled his head down sharply. The movement among the rocks on the far side of the trail had been slight, but it had been accompanied by the brief flash of sunlight off metal, off a gun held in a man's hand.

'Somebody hidin' yonder, on the other side of the trail,' he said, sitting with his shoulders against the tall boulder at his back, eyeing the rest of the men clustered in a tight group near him. 'Better spread out along the ledge here and keep your eyes open for the train when it starts to move in. That's when the trouble is likely to start.'

The men nodded grimly. Tracey watched as they crawled away to take up their position. He remained where he was, crouched behind the boulder, the Winchester in his hands. This time, he thought grimly, the outlaws were due for a big surprise. They would be down there among the rocks, fondly imagining that they had only to do exactly as they had on previous occasions and they would be able to kill off everyone in the wagons, take the gold and ride back to their hideout. There was a growing tension in him as he lay there, waiting. This was going to be the hardest bit, he reflected, not only for him but for the rest of the men. They would be imagining their wagons rolling nearer to the valley between the bluffs and the urge to open fire, even if only to warn those in the wagons, would be a strong thing in them, and yet he had impressed on them all the need to hold their fire until he gave the word. They had to see where the outlaws were hidden, they had to have targets at which to aim, before they could give away their presence.

The sun poured its heat and glaring light on the rocks. There was little shade, not with the sun so high into the sky, fast climbing up to its zenith. Easing his legs out a little in front of him, Tracey tried to shift his body into a more comfortable position, but the rocks were hard and hot under him and the sweat had soaked into his clothing so that it stuck to his back, chafing him with every move he made. He wondered if the other men were suffering as he was and guessed that they were.

Tracey felt dehydrated and tired. The sun had climbed so high now that there were no shadows. He pushed himself up a little, narrowed his eyes as he peered towards the east. At first, he could see no sign of the wagon train. Then he lowered his gaze and saw with a faint thrill that it was now less than a quarter of a mile from the entrance of the trail into the bluffs, the lead wagon rolling forward ponderously, the others strung out behind it. Carefully, he lifted his head and looked down the slope in front of him, guessing that the outlaws would be far too busy watching the approach of the train to bother looking up over their heads at any danger that might exist there.

There was a flash of light, reflected sunlight almost immediately below him and then another. He sucked in a sharp intake of air as he recognized what they were. The men down there were edging their guns in position, ready to open fire and flay those wagons with bullets the minute Carrico or Laredo, whichever man was leading them, gave the order. He tried to make out where these men were, guessing that they would be a little removed from the rest of the outlaw gang. The difficulty, he thought, was going to be those men on the far side of the canyon. Too far away for a Colt to hit them with certainty, it would need a rifle to get in a killing shot.

The leading wagon drove into the canyon. He could clearly hear the clatter of iron shod hooves on the hard rocky floor and the sharp yell from Roberts as he lashed at the horses, urging them on at a faster rate. All the actions of a man who guessed there was trouble here and knew he could do very little about it, beyond driving through as quickly as possible.

A long, breathless pause. Tracey felt his flesh beginning to crawl as if a million red-hot pins were being thrust into it. Would the outlaws never open fire and give away their positions?

Then, with a suddenness that was so startling it took him almost completely by surprise, a solitary shot rang out. It came from a little to his right and in that precise moment, he saw the swift movement as the man leaned forward a little further to aim at the wagons, sighting his rifle on them. Without pausing, Tracey aimed his Winchester, felt the rifle buck against his wrists as he squeezed off the first shot. He saw the man stagger as the bullet hit him between the shoulder blades, then the outlaw pitched forward at a crazy angle over the rocks as they struck him in the chest, sending him hurtling down the slope in a flurry of arms and legs.

The rest of the outlaws continued to fire for several moments, evidently unaware that they had been dry-gulched from behind. Tracey saw other shapes now as the men below tried to better their aim, showing themselves to anyone above them, knowing that they were safe from the fire below. Again and again, the Winchester bucked in his hands as he loosed off half a dozen shots in as many seconds and each time his bullet found its mark, killing or wounding. The wagons had ground to a halt and rifle fire was coming from them, steady and accurate, crashing into the rocks lower down the slopes of the bluffs. Reloading quickly, Tracey squinted along the sights, aiming for the shapes he could just see on the far side of the canyon, men running from one boulder to another, slowly working their way down the slope in their efforts to get closer to the wagon train. He remembered the burning brands which had been used the last time, knew in his heart that those men had to be stopped. Although it was almost at the limit of the range of the Winchester, he saw four men stagger under the hammer blows of the slugs in their bodies. The Winchester was taking its toll now. From further along the ridge, the other men were firing down on the outlaws, their fire cutting gaps in their ranks. This time, there was no doubt that the cards had fallen for them. Caught between two fires, the outlaws continued to shoot it out for several more minutes and then they broke and fled away into the rocks.

Swiftly, Tracey fired two rapid shots into the air, signalling to the rest of the men. Down below, the outlaws were racing for their horses. This was something they had never anticipated, had taken them utterly by surprise. Vaguely, Tracey heard someone yelling savagely at them, guessed that it was either Laredo or Carrico, trying to steady them, force them to stand their ground. But more than half of their number had been slain in this sudden and unexpected attack from above and behind.

'Get back to the horses,' Tracey called. 'They're tryin' to get away.'

'Why don't we let 'em?' growled one of the men. 'Ain't no sense stickin' our necks out now that the wagon train is safe.'

There was a dull rumble of agreement from the other men. 'We didn't agree to come with you to go hunting 'em down in those swamps where they're supposed to have their hideout,' grunted another. 'I'm goin' to ride back to the train. Now that they're on the run and they know we can beat 'em when we try, we'll have no more trouble from them along the trail.'

'Don't be such a lot of goshdarned fools,' Tracey answered harshly. 'Once they've regrouped their forces, they'll hit you again and the next time it will be them who take you by surprise and the boot will be on the other foot.' But his arguments, his pleadings, were to no avail. The men had made up their minds on this point. They had seen the outlaws fleeing from the rocks, and guessed that the wagon train was now perfectly safe from attack. Nothing was going to make them change their minds.

Tightening his lips, Tracey watched them stumble down the slope to where the horses were tethered at the bottom. He followed swiftly, pulled his mount out from the others, thrust the Winchester into the scabbard and swung up into the saddle. His look of scorn failed to shame them, and they did not glance up at him as he wheeled his horse sharply, with a look of black anger on his face, heading out away from the bluffs to the hills in the west, giving his horse its head. He had half expected this. The men would follow him so long as they firmly believed they were protecting their families, but once they had the outlaws on the run and half of them killed or wounded among the rocks, they considered their job was over. They failed to see beyond the present moment, to the time when Carrico would be able to round up his men and force them to move against the wagon train once more, and the next time he would lay his plans well.

He caught the dust drag in his nostrils, lifted by the outlaws as they headed west and once, topping a low rise, he caught a glimpse of the yellow-white cloud in the distance that marked their position. This was a senseless quest on which he had embarked, he knew. There was really nothing that one man could do once those outlaws trailed into the swamps. There they would be on their own ground, would have every advantage and would be able to pick him off whenever they chose. Certainly they would never allow him to get back out of the bayou if he did succeed in trailing them to their secret hideout.

As yet he had no plan in his mind. He had the Winchester it was true, but did that give him the edge over these men? Somehow, he doubted it. On the edge of the swamps, where the sluggish river meandered in a wide turn across country, he fought his way over some of the roughest terrain he had ever known. Progress was slow and the anger and need for revenge that was driving him, made him want to urge the horse forward at a quicker pace as he visualised the outlaws getting so far ahead of him that he would lose them in the swamps.

But reason told him that the ground would slow them just as much as it did him and when he finally came out of it, he picked up their trail quite easily where they had ridden down to the water's edge and put their horses into the water. They had not bothered to mask their emergence from the water on the other bank, clearly confident that they had not been followed. Their trail led into the soft muddy swamps, with thick, poisonous green bushes and vegetation growing in lush profusion on all sides. No wonder these men were able to laugh at the law, hiding in a place such as this. It reminded him of the swamps of Louisiana which he had know as a boy and accordingly, he felt no fear of being in there, trusting his mount to pick its way forward in safety, knowing that the horse had a better instinct that he had for something like this. Once, deep in the bayou, he paused, certain that he heard a noise behind him. He sat quite still in the saddle, ears straining to pick out any sound at all, but now there was only the muted sighing of the breeze through the sloping branches and leaves and in the end, he went on again, making no sound as he brushed aside the feathery growths that reached down in front of him, barring his way at every turn.

He was on top of the hide-out almost before he was aware of it. The trees parted and he found himself staring into the wide clearing where the ground was evidently firmer than elsewhere. He made to move forward, then reined up on the horse and leaned forward with a quick movement, pinching the horse's nostrils as he caught sight of the horses tethered outside the shacks, covered roofs and walls of fern and leaves, forming an almost perfect camouflage against the background.

One of the ponies against the nearest shack suddenly lifted its head and gave a high whinney as it scented his own mount. Tracey waited with the fear and apprehension crowding in to him. Would that sound pass unnoticed, or would someone come out of the shack to see what had caused it? A moment later, the door of the shack opened and a man stepped out into the clearing. He went over to the horses, said something in a low undertone, running his hand over the animal's coat, then he cast a quick look all about him before going back inside.

Tracey let his breath go in slow, short pinches through his nostrils. That had been a closer thing than he had expected. Moving slowly and silently, he led the horse deeper into the trees, tethered it to one of the branches where there was a plentiful supply of lush, deep-green grass, then edged back towards the clearing, holding the Winchester in both hands. There was a coldness on his face and in his body and all of his feelings and senses seemed to have become magnified as though he could pick out fainter sounds than he had thought possible. There was the faint murmur of conversation inside the largest of the shacks. Sounds of argument after a moment, with a man's harsh voice raised loudly above the rest.

Dropping on to his hands and knees, he edged forward, keeping his head and shoulders well down. Maybe if he could get them all hemmed inside that building, he might have a chance of holding them off especially with the Winchester. He wasn't sure how many men were still alive. He reckoned they had killed about a score or more back in the bluffs. That meant there were possibly ten or a dozen of them here. He felt a dull sinking feeling in the pit of his stomach, a feeling that refused to go away no matter how hard he tried to ignore it. He was finished now for sure, he thought, the certainty hammering away at the back of his brain. One man couldn't hope to fight off this bunch of professional killers.

'I tell you we never had a chance, Carrico,' said a man harshly. 'They jumped us from behind before we knew they were there.'

'So you turned and ran like a bunch of yellow-livered cowards,' snapped a deeper voice, which Tracey took to be Carrico's, the real leader of this band.

'What did you expect us to do?' muttered the first man. 'Stick around there and get shot to pieces? I keep tellin' you that Blaine was shot sometime durin' the night. He never had a chance to warn us about this *hombre*, Dillman, who was with that last train. We shouldn't have left him still alive the last time.'

'Don't you reckon you're just tryin' to find excuses for yourselves?' There was a note of angry menace in Carrico's voice now. 'And where is this wagon train now? You've let it slip through your fingers and by now, it'll be well through the bluffs and out into open country where we don't have a chance of takin' them by surprise.'

'We can always hit 'em at the river. That was what I suggested in the first place and—'

'I'll do the plannin' around here,' roared Carrico. 'Everythin' would be fine if I could only trust the men I send out to do the job. We'd have finished that train and the gold would've been in our hands by now if you hadn't turned and run.'

'Now just hold on there.' There was a new note in the other man's voice. 'Nobody's goin' to call me a coward and get away with it. You've been mighty big for a while, givin' all of the orders. But I notice you weren't there to face those bullets. I ain't takin' no more orders from you. Carrico.'

'No? Then draw, damn you. Draw!'

A moment's pause. A split second in which there seemed to be no movement. Even to the man crouched outside the shack, everything seemed to stand still in that second. Then there came the crash of two shots, so close together that they sounded like one. Scarcely had the atrophying echoes died away than he made out the crash of a falling body inside the shack. The voice he knew to be Carrico's said harshly. 'Get that body out of here, unless anyone else wants to make a try.'

There was no answer and scarcely had Tracey crawled out of sight behind a clump of thick brush than the door opened and two men staggered out, carrying the body of a man between them. They walked away from the shacks, then dropped the body into the rough grass on the edge of the clearing and walked back towards the hut.

Tracey knew that very soon, he would be seen, that he had to make his move now if he was to gain any advantage of surprise. The two men were hard-faced, cruel killers. He felt no compunction as he laid the sights of the rifle on them and fired twice in rapid succession.

Both men staggered and whirled, as the slugs tore into them. One man dropped where he stood, the other seemed to run back on his toes, strangely off balance before collapsing into the grass. Instantly, there was pandemonium inside the shack. He heard Carrico's voice yelling something inaudible, then there came the crash of glass from one of the windows and the short barrel of a Colt was thrust out, glistening faintly in the dimness of the swamp. Tracey aimed and fired in the same second, heard a yell of pain and the Colt vanished as its owner fell back from the window.

For a moment, there was silence, no movement of any kind inside the shack. Tracey waited tensely. He could not guess what the men in there would do. They had no way of telling how many men might be lying in wait for them outside around the clearing and they would not be wanting to expose themselves to this dangerous and accurate fire which had killed two of their number and wounded a third.

Seconds later, more return fire came from inside the shack. Bullets hammered a tattoo on the soft ground, digging into the mud as they struck all around the spot where Tracey lay hidden. None of them came within a yard of his body and he held his fire until he caught the movement near the door. The man was evidently trying to rush out into the open under covering fire from the others when Tracey loosed off two shots. The first missed, struck the wooden door and buried itself with a faint smack in the wood. But the second found its mark in the fleshy part of the man's belly and he doubled over, falling on to his face into the dirt just outside the door. Somebody grabbed him by the ankles and hauled him back inside and Tracey heard the thin, high-pitched screams of him as he died slowly and in agony.

Now the flash from his Winchester had been seen and the return fire became more accurate and deadly. He was forced to push himself further into the ground to present a small target and there was the splintering of branches over his head as the volley tore through the air just above him. More glass shattered from one of the other windows, the ugly snouts of revolvers poked through and he heard the wicked hum of slugs tearing through the air close to his head. For a moment he had a creepy feeling about it, felt a second of panic as fear ate its way into his brain. He was pinned down here, unable to move backward or forward without exposing himself to their fire. The savage destruction shook him to the very roots of his courage. He had not imagined that gunfire could be so terrible. Something burned a scorching finger along his upper arm. He glanced down, saw that there was blood on his sleeve, but when he flexed the fingers of that arm he found to his surprise that he was able to move them and knew that the bullet had torn the skin without affecting the bone or the nerves. He aimed the Winchester, fired shot after shot through the window nearest him, working the mechanism easily and swiftly. Then the gun was empty and he rolled over on to one side, careful not to expose himself more than was necessary and pulled the Colts from their holsters.

Once they were empty, he was finished. He knew that it would not be long before the men holed up in that shack realized that they were being played for suckers, that there was only one man facing them and they had only to slip out and take him from two sides and he was done, finished.

The firing swung round. Most of it was coming from the direction of the door of the shack. He guessed at the reason for this at once, even before Carrico's bull-like yell from inside the shack.

'All right, men. There's only one hombre out there. It's probably Dillman with that fancy rifle of his. Go out and get him. We'll cover you from the window.'

A man broke out of the shack, ran from the doorway, paused for a moment looking about him, then dropped under cover. Tracey sent a shot at the place where he had gone to earth, but it was impossible to tell whether the bullet had found its mark or not. He knew with a sickening certainty that he must surely be finished now. It had been a foolish thing he had done anyway, trailing them here and hoping to finish them himself. He ought to have gone back with this knowledge and informed the Major of what he had found; that way it might be possible for—

His thoughts broke off, gelled in his head. A volley of fire crashed out from the ring of vegetation surrounding the clearing. He heard it smash with a terrible sound into the walls of the shack, heard the yells of the men inside, heard death come to someone as a tearing impact of lead passing through cloth and then flesh and bone, followed by the grunt and sigh of air passing out of the dying man's lungs. Every muscle in Tracey's body was so tight that he began to ache. At first he could not comprehend what was happening. His first thought that perhaps he had really shamed those men into riding after him, was soon dismissed. They would be back at the wagon train by now and nothing would induce them to leave it.

Then he threw a quick glance over his shoulder, caught a glimpse of blue against the green of the foliage and knew what had happened, knew that the Major had received word of the wagon train moving out of New Orleans and had somehow managed to pick up his trail, following him into the bayou. A second later, he heard the other's sharp yell:

'Get back here among the trees, Dillman. We'll cover you.'

He scrambled back with great heaves of his arms and legs, still gripping the rifle in his right hand. A volley crashed out from the trees, was answered by another from the shack as Carrico's harsh voice yelled a further order. Somehow, he managed to gain the comparative safety of the trees, turned to find the Major beside him.

'So you did manage to track me,' he said in a harsh breath.

The other nodded. 'We spotted you harin' off to the west after those critters and once we'd made sure that the wagon train was safe, we cut out after you.'

'Glad you did. I was sure in trouble there.'

'What happened to Laredo?' queried the other. 'Don't see him around.'

'There was a quarrel and Carrico shot him inside the shack. They've dumped his body yonder on the edge of the clearing. We won't have to bother about him any more and Carrico is holed up in the shack.'

The Major turned, grim-visaged and signalled his men to move forward. Tracey saw that the troops were spread out around the entire clearing so that there was to be no escape for any of the outlaws. They had fled from the wagon train when they had been attacked, and in their panic, they had led not only him, but the military to their hideout and now they were paying the price of their folly.

The firing swung around to the rear of the shack and Tracey picked out the yells as men who had been trying to slip away from the back were caught in the open and cut down. Suddenly, the door of the shack burst open and two men came running out, their hands held high over their heads.

'Hold your fire, men,' called the Major. 'Those two men want to surrender.'

The two men had only taken a couple of paces however, when there came the sound of two shots, close together from the dimness inside the shack. Tracey caught a brief glimpse of the red stabbing tongues of flames. Then both men threw up their arms as they were shot in the back and fell mortally wounded.

'Nobody runs out on me,' roared Carrico harshly. He lifted his voice a little to be heard by everyone. 'If you want me, soldier-boys, you'll have to come in and get me, and I'll take plenty of you with me.'

'There can't be many more men alive in there with him,' Tracey said swiftly. He lifted his head and threw a swift glance into the half open door. He could make out nothing that moved, and there was only the body of the man he had shot and who had been dragged inside by his heels, lying in the doorway just inside the shack. Carrico was evidently hiding well inside, not showing himself, but ready to open fire if they decided to rush the place.

'We'll have to go in and take him,' he said after a contemplative pause. 'It's the only way. He could hold out for long enough if we don't.'

The Major gave a quick shake of his head. 'It will be sheer suicide to try to get inside there,' he said sharply.

'I'm willin' to try it,' Tracey muttered. He felt the dull anger still at work within him, knew that he would not rest until this man, who was behind all of the robbing and killing, was dead.

'You're a fool if you do,' said the other, but Tracey thought he detected a faint trace of grudging admiration in his tone. 'But like I said to you once before, you're a civilian and I can't give you any orders.'

'Then keep me covered until I work my way to one of those windows,' Tracey said tersely. He checked the Winchester, thrusting a fresh slip of cartridges into the stock, filled the Colts from his belt, then slithered forward through the tall grass, listening to the rapid bark of the rifles from behind him as the men opened fire to cover his progress. The dull hammering of his heart against his ribs was so loud in his ears he felt certain that Carrico would hear it even above the sound of the guns. He reached the bodies of the two men Carrico had shot in the back, moved around them slowly, careful to make no noise.

Dimly, he was aware of the thudding of the bullets into the thick walls of the shack. They were a good protection for anyone hiding inside, the walls built of thick logs which would take a bullet easily and absorb it. A man could lie behind those walls without fear of being hit.

An occasional shot came from inside the shack, and he could hear the other moving around inside as he fired from one window after the other in turn. It was not going to be easy to get close enough to take Carrico, but he had committed himself now and there was to be no turning back. Only ten yards to go now and he would reach the shack wall.

His breath was rasping in his throat as he finally rose up from the grass close to the side of the shack. If there were other men still inside there, alive and ready to continue the fight, either because they knew that they would be hanged once the Major took them, or because Carrico had shown in the clearest possible manner that he would shoot down any man who tried to give himself up, then his life might be forfeit. He would not be able to watch two men, certainly not if one of them was a fast gunman like Carrico.

Getting to his feet aware that the firing had swung to

cover the front of the shack and hoping that Carrico would not tumble immediately to the reason for this, he pressed himself tightly against the wall and began to edge his way towards the window. There was further movement inside the shack. He stood close beside the window for several moments, like a man thoroughly exhausted, scarcely able to move or control the slight trembling in his body.

Pulling one of the Colts from its holster, he stepped forward, reached the window and thrust the barrel of the Colt inside. In the gloom inside the shack, he made out the bodies on the wooden floor behind the windows where they had been cut down either by his initial fire or that from the troops. Then he saw Carrico. The other stood with his back to him, close to the door, a couple of Colts in his hands.

For a moment, nothing seemed to exist, but that one man. Then Tracey said very softly. 'All right, Carrico. Freeze!'

The other stiffened, he saw the faint movement of the man's shoulder blades under the thin shirt, the way his arms were tensed by his sides.

'Drop those guns and move out of the shack with your hands lifted,' he said tightly. 'I'll give you three seconds and then shoot you in the back. And if you figure I won't, I'll tell you that I was with that last wagon train you massacred.'

'Tracey Dillman.' There was a coldly sardonic tone to the other's voice. He did not seem to have any fear at the fact that there was clearly a gun laid on him.

'That's right. *Now drop those guns.*'

A pause while the other seemed to be contemplating the order. Then, without warning, he whirled, the guns lifting to cover the window. Tracey fired, felt the wind of a bullet fan his cheek. Then Carrico lurched forward, his hands drooping. The guns in his fists went off again with the last ounce of strength in his body, kicking up great gouts of splintered wood from the floor at the outlaw's feet. For a moment, he remained upright, trying to keep life in his eyes, shocked unbelief on his swarthy features, striving to get the strength into his arms to enable him to lift his Colts and line up the barrels on Tracey's chest. But his knees buckled and a moment later, all of the starch went out of him and he fell over the inert body of the man lying just inside the doorway, the guns flying from nerveless fingers, clattering on to the floor.

It was all over. The outlaw band had been smashed and broken. As they rode back in the direction of the trail, Tracey felt a little of the feeling come back into his tired body. This was a day he had never thought to see, when this first great obstacle along the trail west to California would be removed. Now the bluffs would be open to other wagon trains moving west. There would be more dangers to face, flood and desert, Indian tribes on the warpath and more outlaws lying in wait for them. But they had shown that these outcasts from decent society could be faced and beaten.

'We'll leave you at the wagon train,' said the Major, as they rode out of the swamps and along the bank of the wide river. 'I expect you'll be wanting to rejoin them and head out for California.'

'That's right,' Tracey nodded. 'There's a whole new country out there waiting to be claimed and I aim to be in on it at the beginning, get myself a bit of land and set my roots down there.'

'It sounds good,' admitted the other. 'I had kind of hoped I might be able to persuade you to stick around these parts, maybe act as scout for us. We need good men with a rifle like you, men we can trust. We have to open up this stretch of the frontier too, you know, to keep the wagon trains moving through on their way. We're playing our part in opening up this continent.'

He turned his quiet eyes on Tracey, regarding him seriously for a long moment, but the other shook his head. 'Thanks for the offer, Major,' he said soberly. 'If things had been a mite different, I'd have been glad and honoured to accept your offer. But I've made up my mind. I want to see California and see if it's as good as they say it is. It might be that I'm not taken to it and if that's the case, well then, I reckon I'll come back this way and see if that offer is still open.'

'It will be, as long as I'm commander of the outpost,' declared the other. They swung around a bend in the trail and there in front of them lay the wagon train, moving slowly across the lush green land, in single file, horses and oxen pulling in the traces, a part of the population of the country, heading west into a land of new promise, west into the red sunset that painted a line of flaming red across the peaks of the distant hills.

The other shook hands with him, then raised his right hand in a stiff military salute, barked a command at the men, and they rode off to the north-east, back to the outpost. Tracey sat watching them go for a long moment, feeling as if a part of him were going away with them. Then he swung his mount and put it to a steady lope towards the wagons.

It would possibly take them six months before they crossed this vast continent and went into California, but now he had the strange certainty that whatever happened on the way, they would make it now. For a moment, he leaned forward in the saddle and ran his fingers, almost caressingly over the stock of the Winchester. Soon, there would be hordes of men and women following them, a great people heading west, breaking the trails which millions would follow.